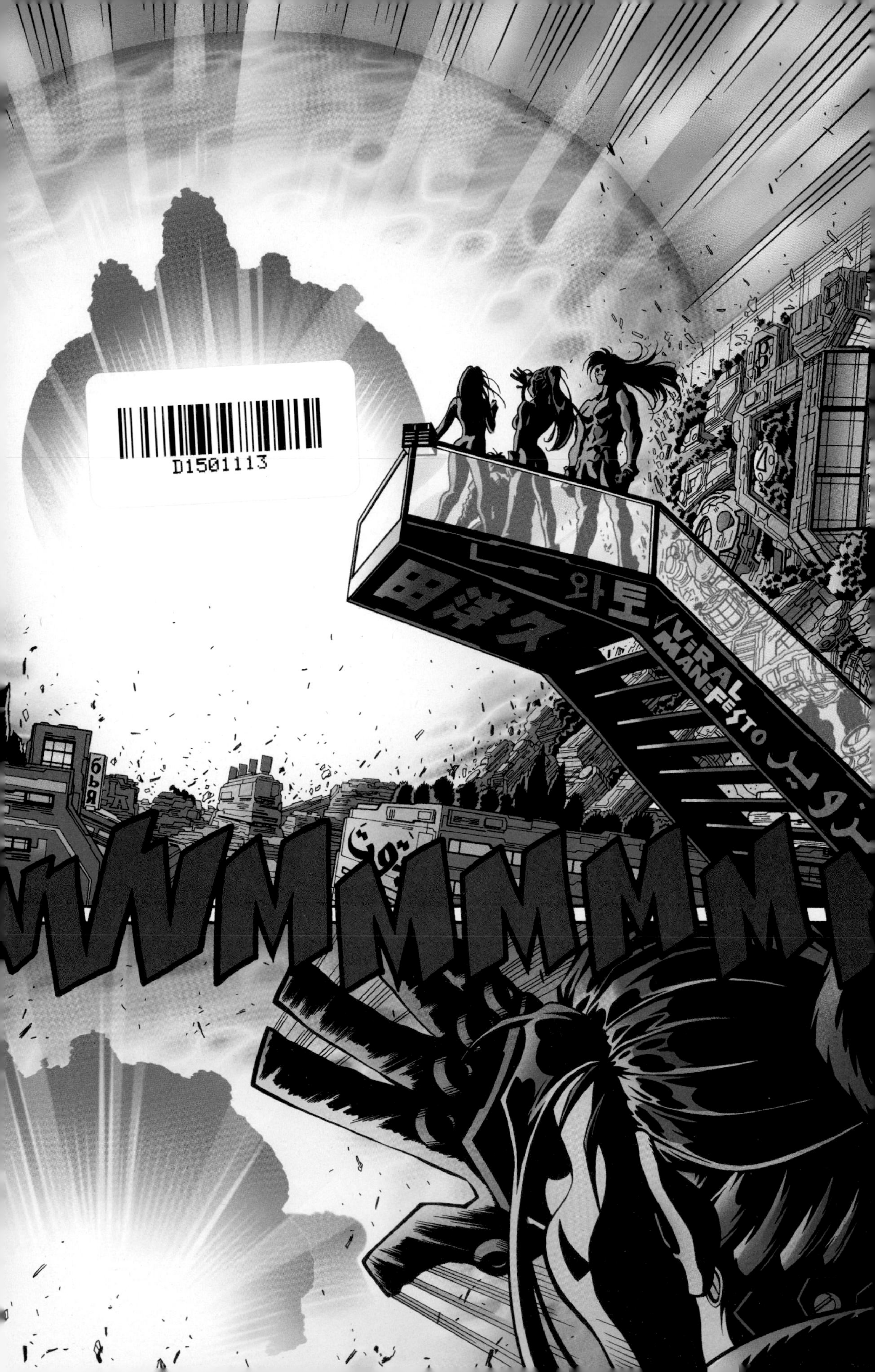
와토
VIRAL MANIFESTO
WVMMMMMM

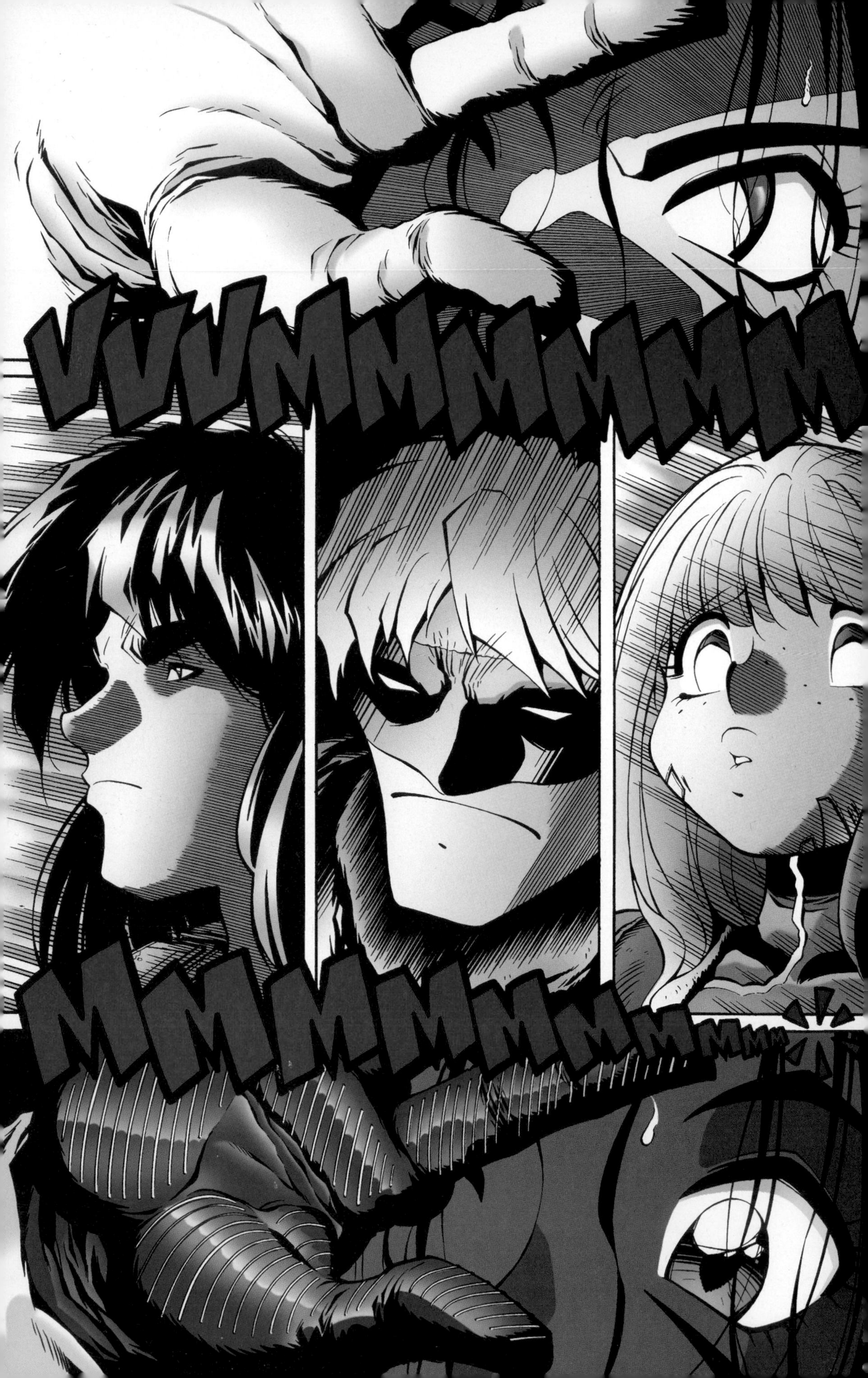
VVVMMMMMMMMM
MMMMMMMMMMMM

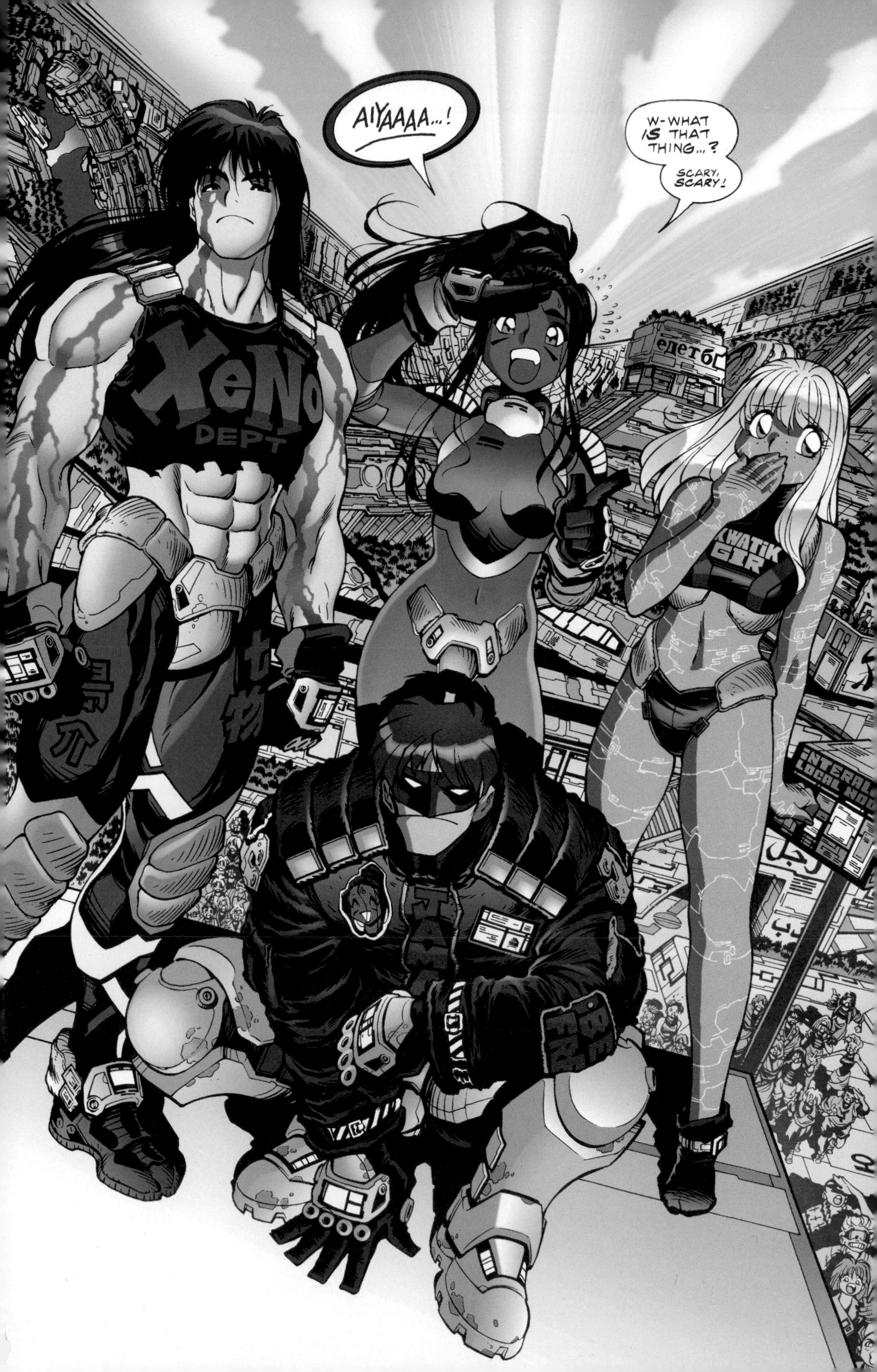
AIYAAAA...!
W-WHAT IS THAT THING...?
SCARY, SCARY!

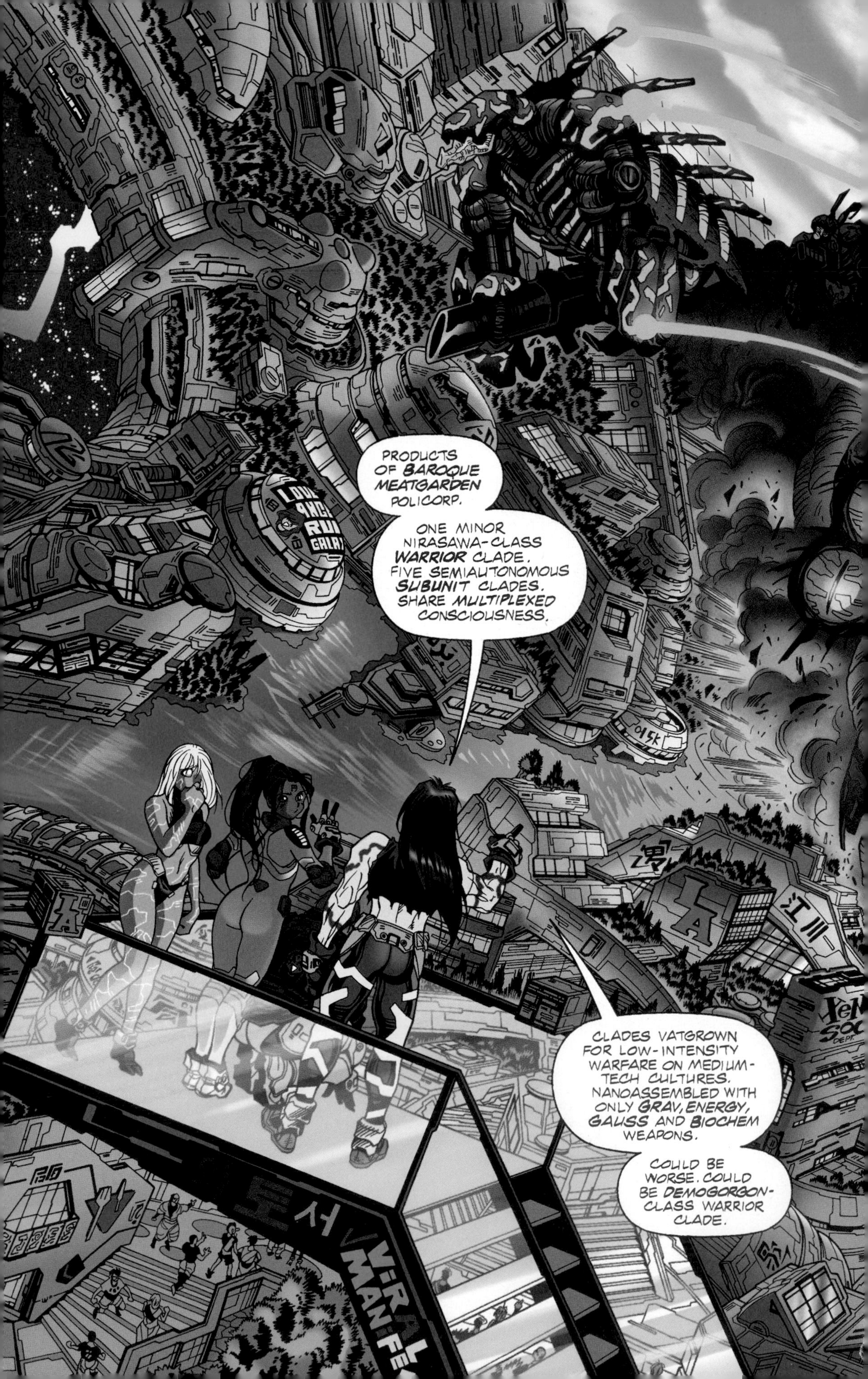
PRODUCTS OF BAROQUE MEATGARDEN POLICORP.
ONE MINOR NIRASAWA-CLASS WARRIOR CLADE. FIVE SEMIAUTONOMOUS SUBUNIT CLADES. SHARE MULTIPLEXED CONSCIOUSNESS.
CLADES VATGROWN FOR LOW-INTENSITY WARFARE ON MEDIUM-TECH CULTURES. NANOASSEMBLED WITH ONLY GRAV, ENERGY, GAUSS AND BIOCHEM WEAPONS.
COULD BE WORSE. COULD BE DEMOGORGON-CLASS WARRIOR CLADE.

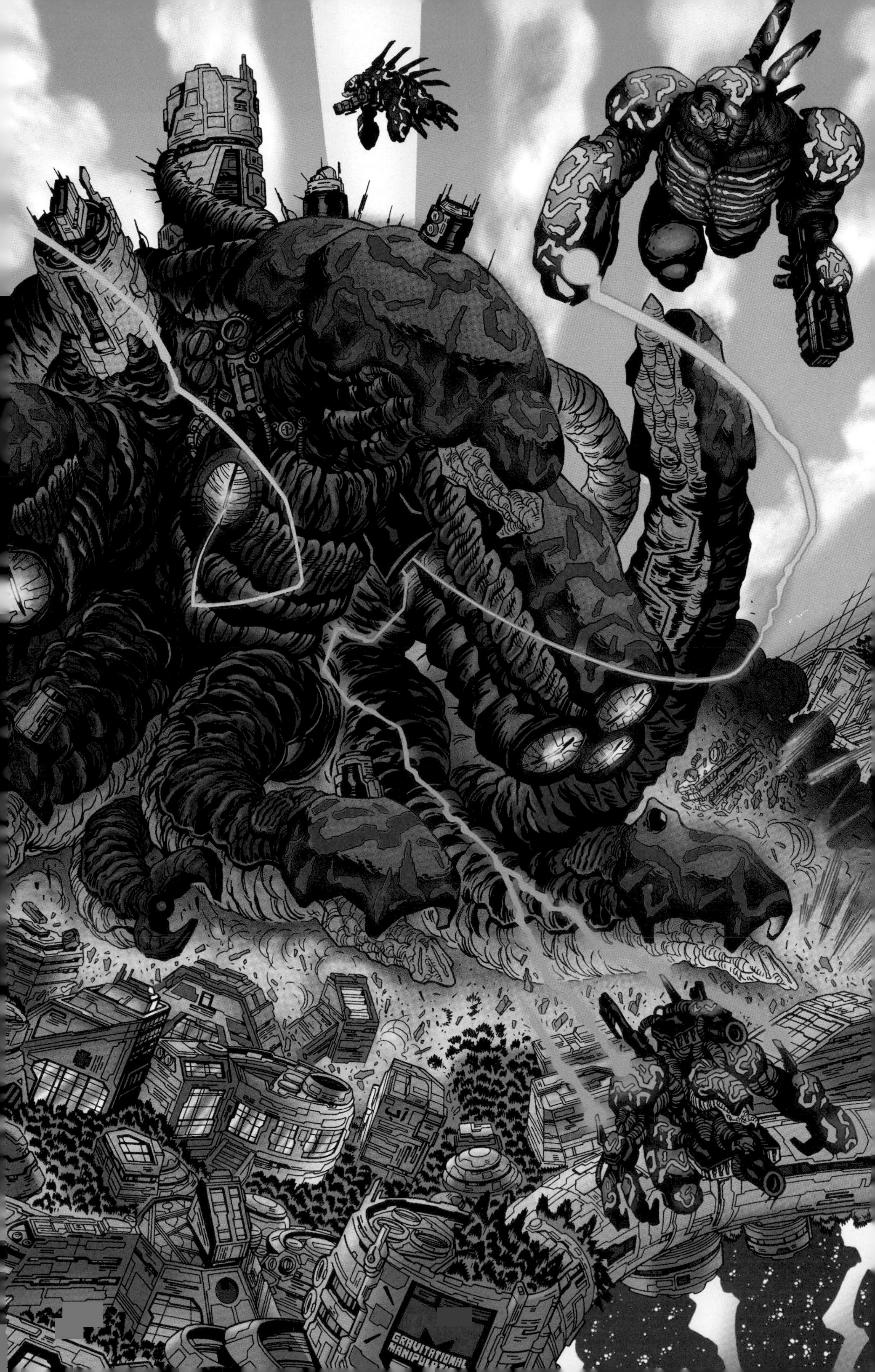
GRAVITATIONAL

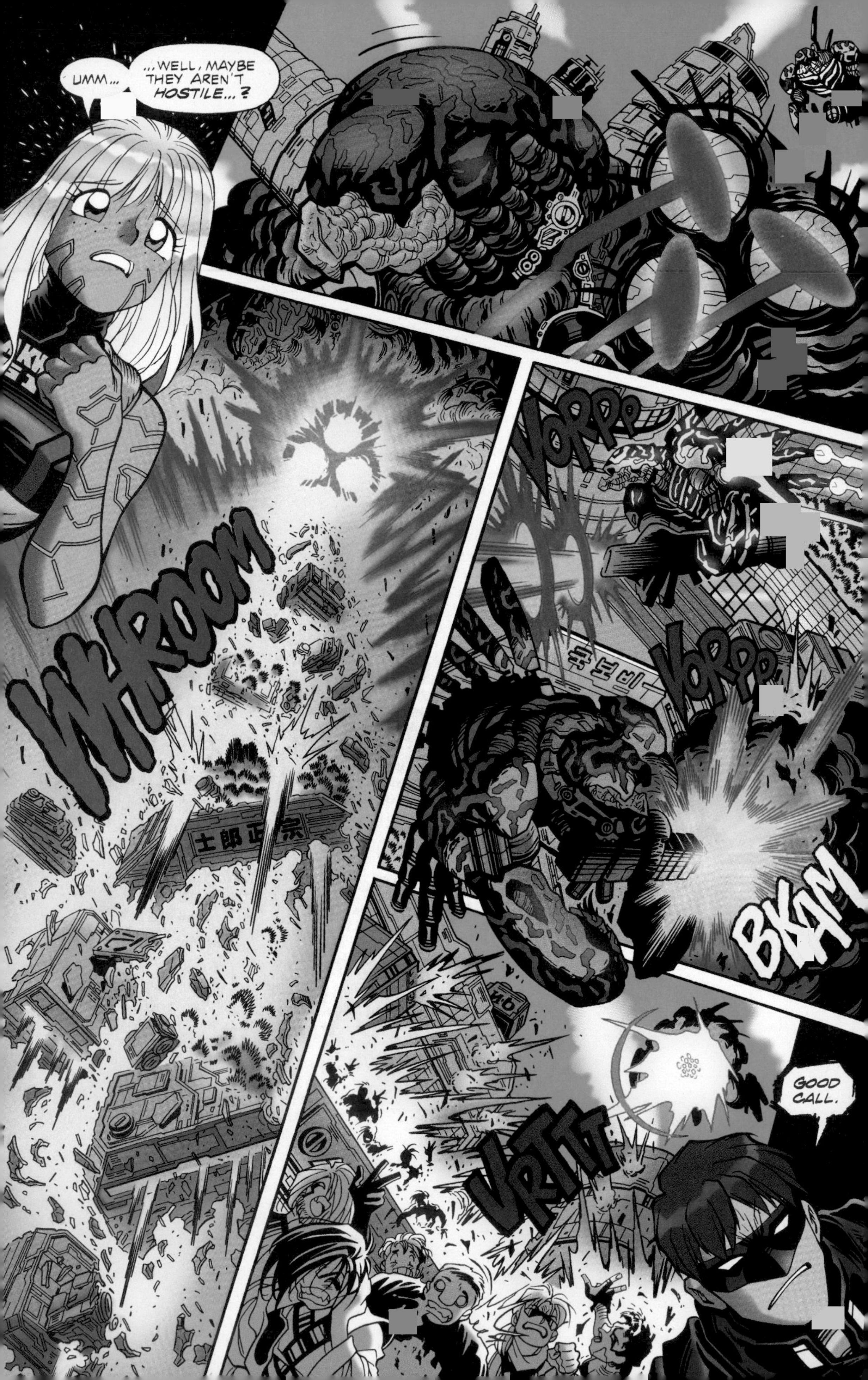
UMM...
...WELL, MAYBE THEY AREN'T HOSTILE...?
WHROOM
士郎正宗
VORPP
VORPP
BKAM
VRTTT
GOOD CALL.

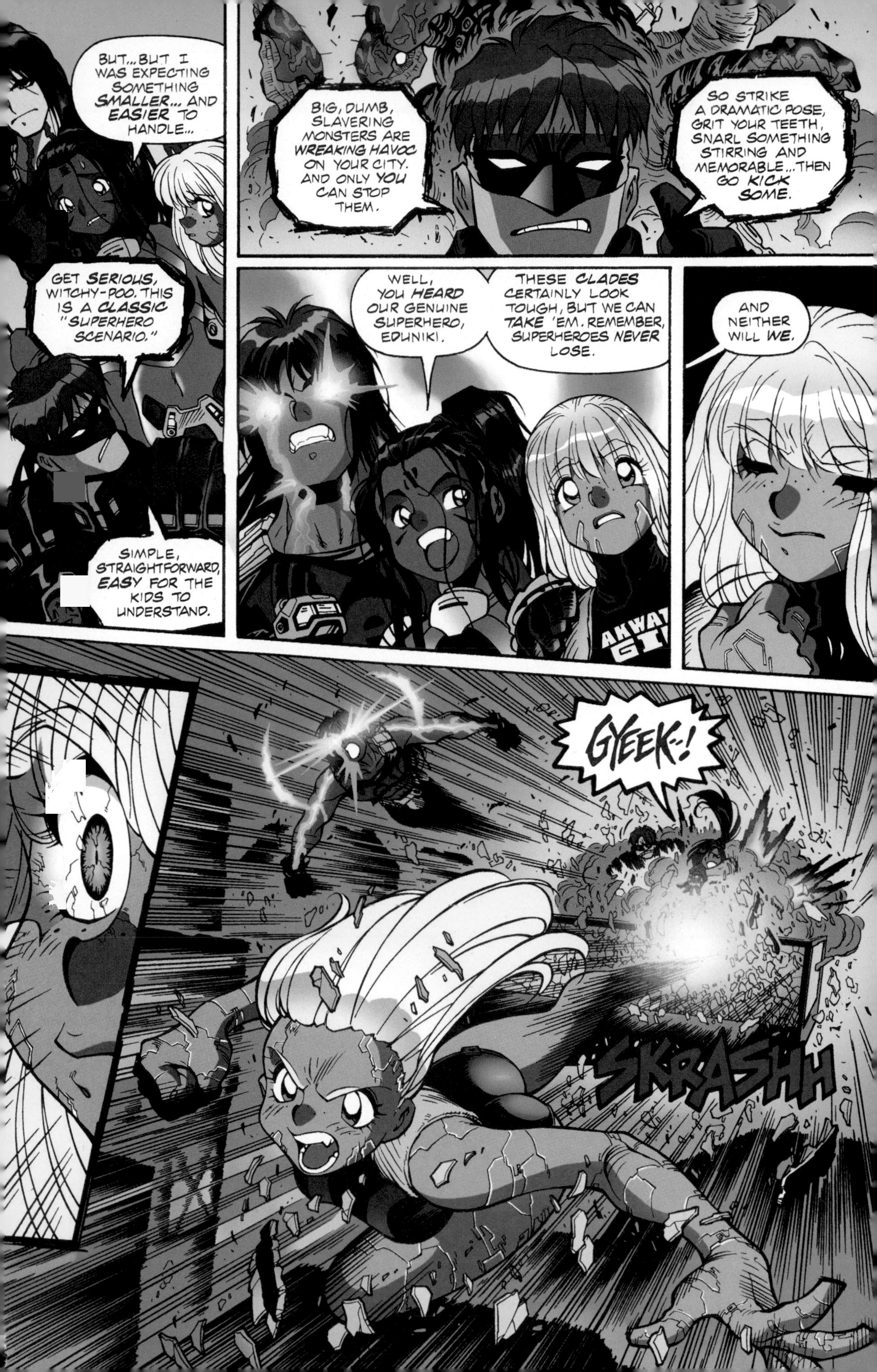
BUT... BUT I WAS EXPECTING SOMETHING SMALLER... AND EASIER TO HANDLE...
GET SERIOUS, WITCHY-POO. THIS IS A CLASSIC "SUPERHERO SCENARIO."
SIMPLE, STRAIGHTFORWARD, EASY FOR THE KIDS TO UNDERSTAND.
BIG, DUMB, SLAVERING MONSTERS ARE WREAKING HAVOC ON YOUR CITY. AND ONLY YOU CAN STOP THEM.
SO STRIKE A DRAMATIC POSE, GRIT YOUR TEETH, SNARL SOMETHING STIRRING AND MEMORABLE... THEN GO KICK SOME.
WELL, YOU HEARD OUR GENUINE SUPERHERO, EDUNIKI.
THESE CLADES CERTAINLY LOOK TOUGH, BUT WE CAN TAKE 'EM. REMEMBER, SUPERHEROES NEVER LOSE.
AND NEITHER WILL WE.
GYEEK--!
SKRASHH

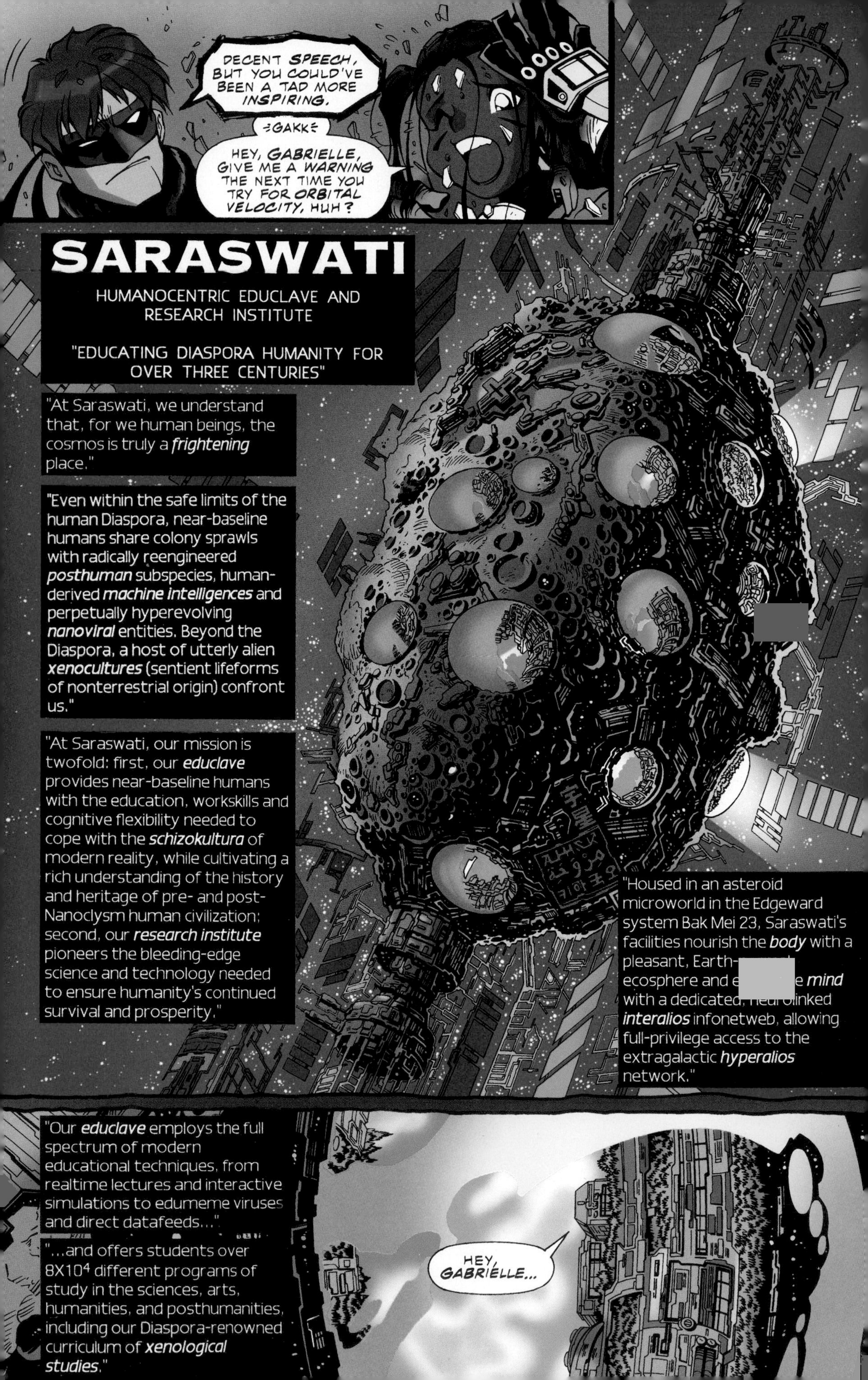
DECENT SPEECH, BUT YOU COULD'VE BEEN A TAD MORE INSPIRING.
=GAKK=
HEY, GABRIELLE, GIVE ME A WARNING THE NEXT TIME YOU TRY FOR ORBITAL VELOCITY, HUH?
SARASWATI
HUMANOCENTRIC EDUCLAVE AND RESEARCH INSTITUTE
"EDUCATING DIASPORA HUMANITY FOR OVER THREE CENTURIES"
"At Saraswati, we understand that, for we human beings, the cosmos is truly a *frightening* place."
"Even within the safe limits of the human Diaspora, near-baseline humans share colony sprawls with radically reengineered *posthuman* subspecies, human-derived *machine intelligences* and perpetually hyperevolving *nanoviral* entities. Beyond the Diaspora, a host of utterly alien *xenocultures* (sentient lifeforms of nonterrestrial origin) confront us."
"At Saraswati, our mission is twofold: first, our *educlave* provides near-baseline humans with the education, workskills and cognitive flexibility needed to cope with the *schizokultura* of modern reality, while cultivating a rich understanding of the history and heritage of pre- and post-Nanoclysm human civilization; second, our *research institute* pioneers the bleeding-edge science and technology needed to ensure humanity's continued survival and prosperity."
"Housed in an asteroid microworld in the Edgeward system Bak Mei 23, Saraswati's facilities nourish the *body* with a pleasant, Earth- ecosphere and e e *mind* with a dedicated, neurolinked *interalios* infonetweb, allowing full-privilege access to the extragalactic *hyperalios* network."
"Our *educlave* employs the full spectrum of modern educational techniques, from realtime lectures and interactive simulations to edumeme viruses and direct datafeeds..."
"...and offers students over 8X10⁴ different programs of study in the sciences, arts, humanities, and posthumanities, including our Diaspora-renowned curriculum of *xenological studies*."
HEY, GABRIELLE...

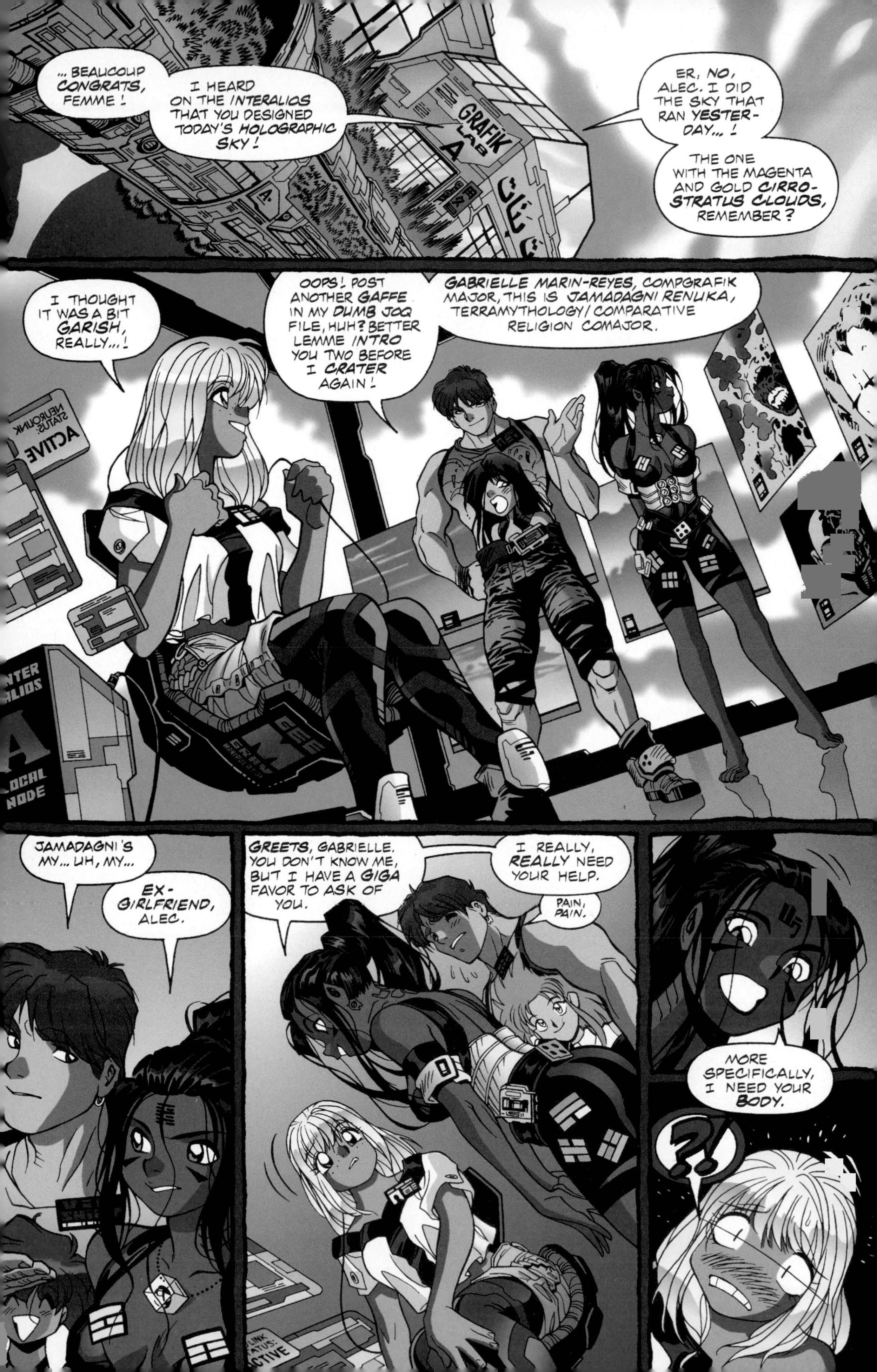

... BEAUCOUP CONGRATS, FEMME!
I HEARD ON THE INTERALIOS THAT YOU DESIGNED TODAY'S HOLOGRAPHIC SKY!
GRAFIK LAB A
ER, NO, ALEC. I DID THE SKY THAT RAN YESTER-DAY... !
THE ONE WITH THE MAGENTA AND GOLD CIRRO-STRATUS CLOUDS, REMEMBER?
I THOUGHT IT WAS A BIT GARISH, REALLY...!
OOPS! POST ANOTHER GAFFE IN MY DUMB JOQ FILE, HUH? BETTER LEMME INTRO YOU TWO BEFORE I CRATER AGAIN!
GABRIELLE MARIN-REYES, COMPGRAFIK MAJOR, THIS IS JAMADAGNI RENUKA, TERRAMYTHOLOGY/COMPARATIVE RELIGION COMAJOR.
NEUROLINK STATUS: ACTIVE
INTER ALIOS A LOCAL NODE
JAMADAGNI'S MY... UH, MY...
EX-GIRLFRIEND, ALEC.
GREETS, GABRIELLE. YOU DON'T KNOW ME, BUT I HAVE A GIGA FAVOR TO ASK OF YOU.
I REALLY, REALLY NEED YOUR HELP.
PAIN, PAIN.
MORE SPECIFICALLY, I NEED YOUR BODY.
?!

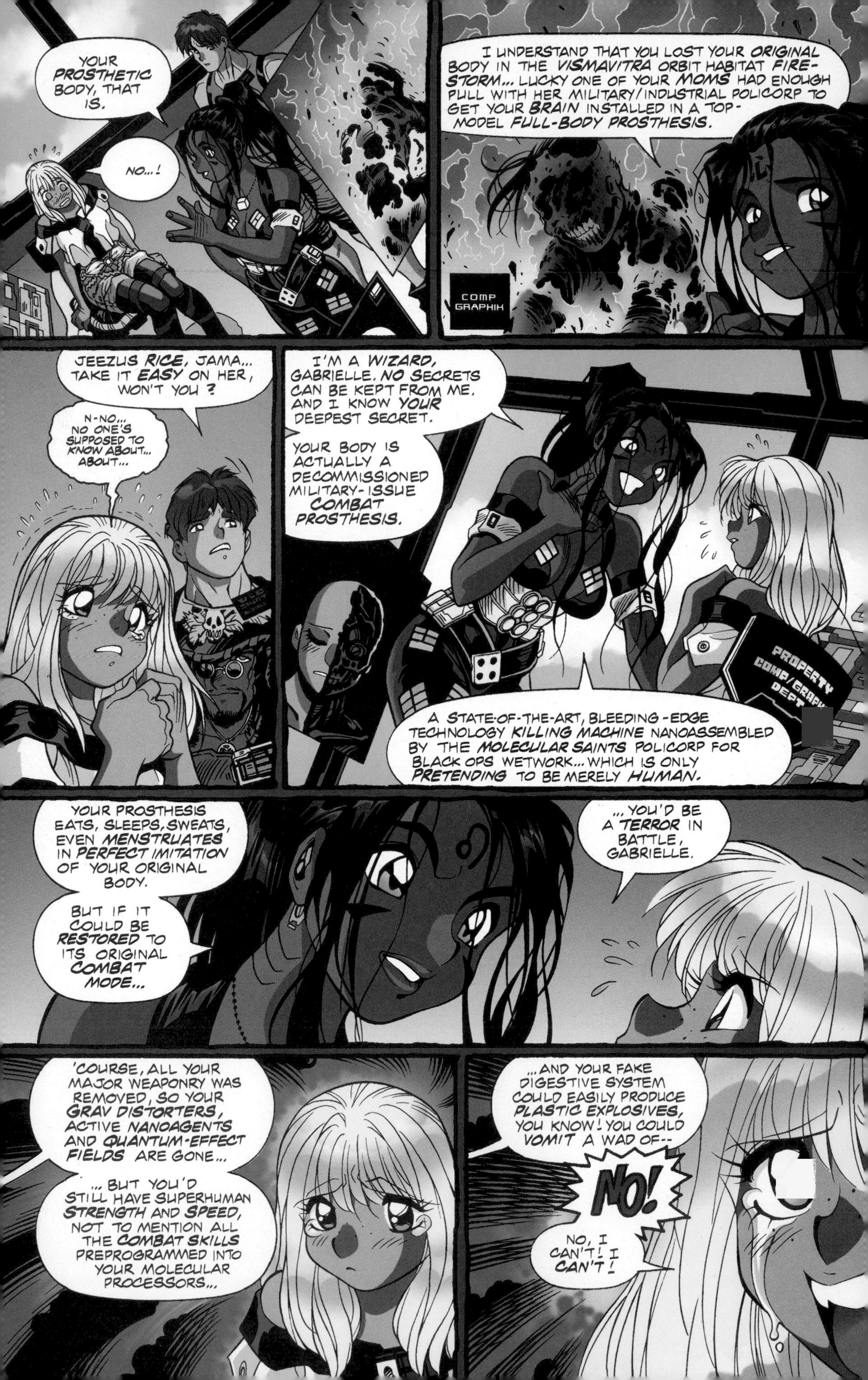
YOUR PROSTHETIC BODY, THAT IS.
NO...!
I UNDERSTAND THAT YOU LOST YOUR ORIGINAL BODY IN THE VISMAVITRA ORBIT HABITAT FIRE-STORM... LUCKY ONE OF YOUR MOMS HAD ENOUGH PULL WITH HER MILITARY/INDUSTRIAL POLICORP TO GET YOUR BRAIN INSTALLED IN A TOP-MODEL FULL-BODY PROSTHESIS.
COMP GRAPHIK
JEEZUS RICE, JAMA... TAKE IT EASY ON HER, WON'T YOU ?
N-NO... NO ONE'S SUPPOSED TO KNOW ABOUT... ABOUT...
I'M A WIZARD, GABRIELLE. NO SECRETS CAN BE KEPT FROM ME. AND I KNOW YOUR DEEPEST SECRET.
YOUR BODY IS ACTUALLY A DECOMMISSIONED MILITARY-ISSUE COMBAT PROSTHESIS.
PROPERTY COMP/GRAPH DEPT
A STATE-OF-THE-ART, BLEEDING-EDGE TECHNOLOGY KILLING MACHINE NANOASSEMBLED BY THE MOLECULAR SAINTS POLICORP FOR BLACK OPS WETWORK... WHICH IS ONLY PRETENDING TO BE MERELY HUMAN.
YOUR PROSTHESIS EATS, SLEEPS, SWEATS, EVEN MENSTRUATES IN PERFECT IMITATION OF YOUR ORIGINAL BODY.
BUT IF IT COULD BE RESTORED TO ITS ORIGINAL COMBAT MODE...
...YOU'D BE A TERROR IN BATTLE, GABRIELLE.
'COURSE, ALL YOUR MAJOR WEAPONRY WAS REMOVED, SO YOUR GRAV DISTORTERS, ACTIVE NANOAGENTS AND QUANTUM-EFFECT FIELDS ARE GONE...
...BUT YOU'D STILL HAVE SUPERHUMAN STRENGTH AND SPEED, NOT TO MENTION ALL THE COMBAT SKILLS PREPROGRAMMED INTO YOUR MOLECULAR PROCESSORS...
...AND YOUR FAKE DIGESTIVE SYSTEM COULD EASILY PRODUCE PLASTIC EXPLOSIVES, YOU KNOW! YOU COULD VOMIT A WAD OF--
NO!
NO, I CAN'T! I CAN'T!

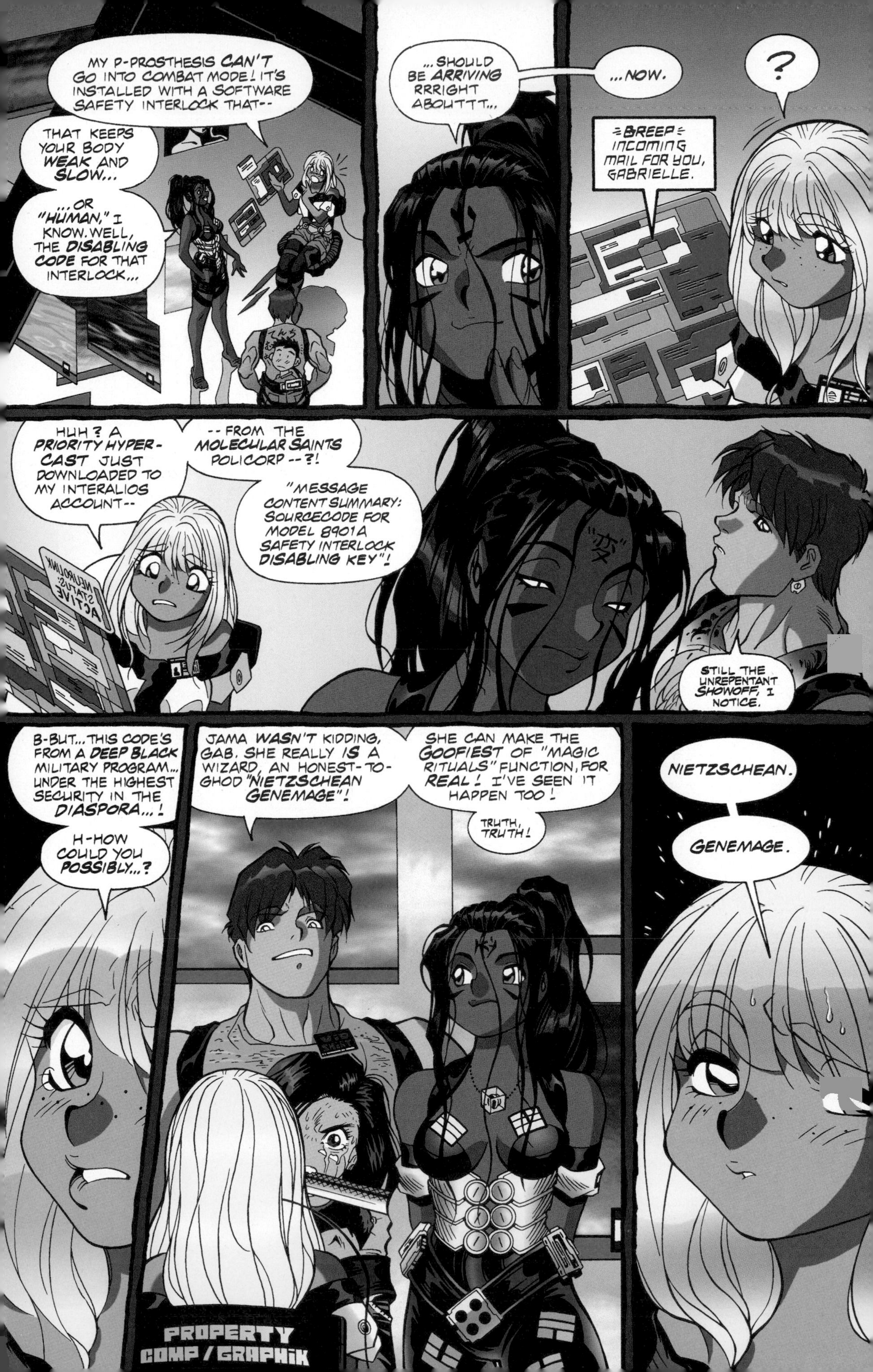

MY P-PROSTHESIS CAN'T GO INTO COMBAT MODE! IT'S INSTALLED WITH A SOFTWARE SAFETY INTERLOCK THAT--
THAT KEEPS YOUR BODY WEAK AND SLOW...
...OR "HUMAN," I KNOW. WELL, THE DISABLING CODE FOR THAT INTERLOCK...
...SHOULD BE ARRIVING RRRIGHT ABOUTTT...
...NOW.
?
=BREEP= INCOMING MAIL FOR YOU, GABRIELLE.
HUH? A PRIORITY HYPER-CAST JUST DOWNLOADED TO MY INTERALIOS ACCOUNT--
--FROM THE MOLECULAR SAINTS POLICORP--?!
"MESSAGE CONTENT SUMMARY: SOURCECODE FOR MODEL 8901A SAFETY INTERLOCK DISABLING KEY"!
"変"
STILL THE UNREPENTANT SHOWOFF, I NOTICE.
B-BUT... THIS CODE'S FROM A DEEP BLACK MILITARY PROGRAM... UNDER THE HIGHEST SECURITY IN THE DIASPORA...!
H-HOW COULD YOU POSSIBLY...?
JAMA WASN'T KIDDING, GAB. SHE REALLY IS A WIZARD, AN HONEST-TO-GHOD "NIETZSCHEAN GENEMAGE"!
SHE CAN MAKE THE GOOFIEST OF "MAGIC RITUALS" FUNCTION, FOR REAL! I'VE SEEN IT HAPPEN TOO!
TRUTH, TRUTH!
NIETZSCHEAN.
GENEMAGE.
PROPERTY COMP / GRAPHIK

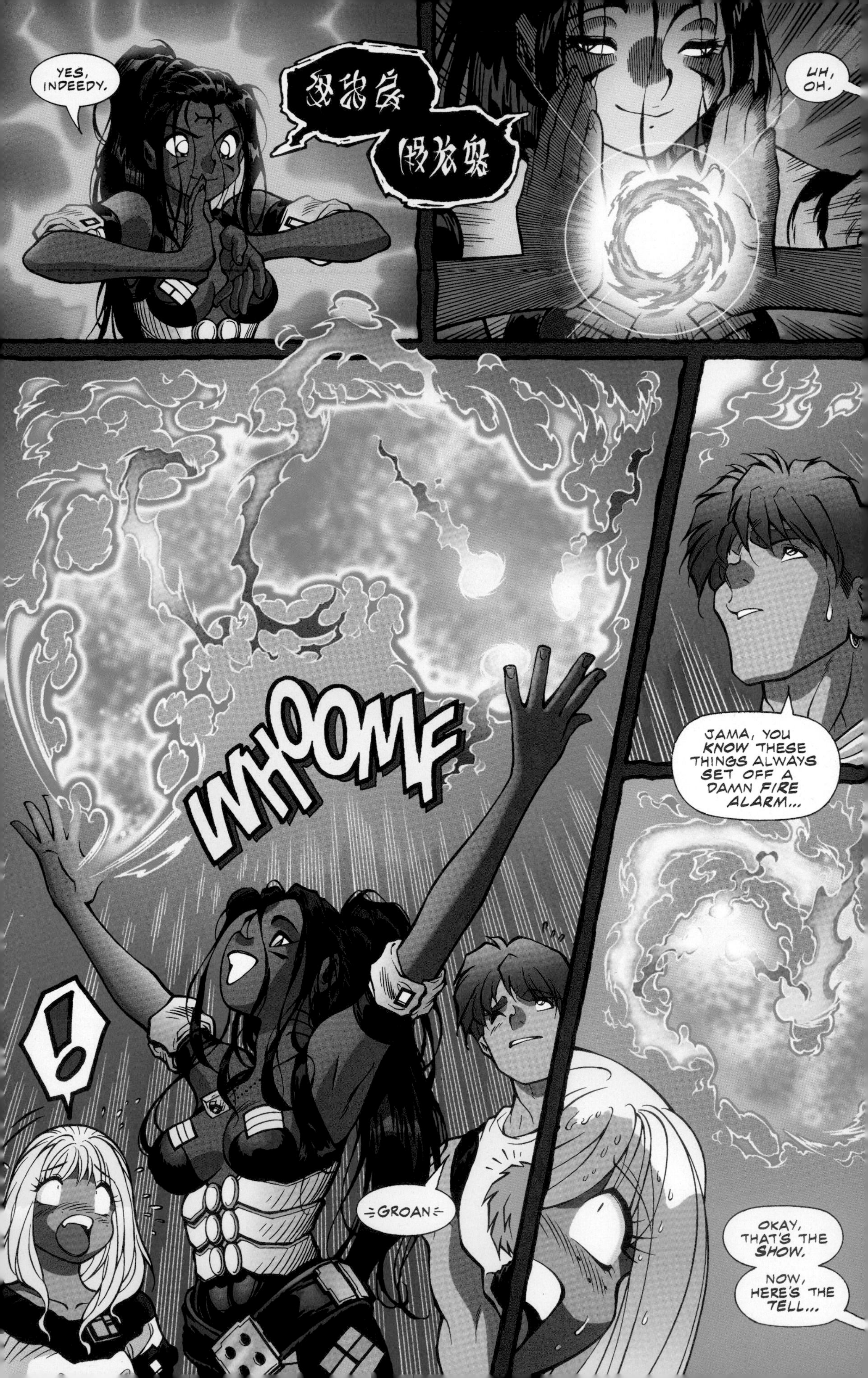

YES, INDEEDY.
UH, OH.
WHOOMF
JAMA, YOU KNOW THESE THINGS ALWAYS SET OFF A DAMN FIRE ALARM...
!
GROAN
OKAY, THAT'S THE SHOW.
NOW, HERE'S THE TELL...

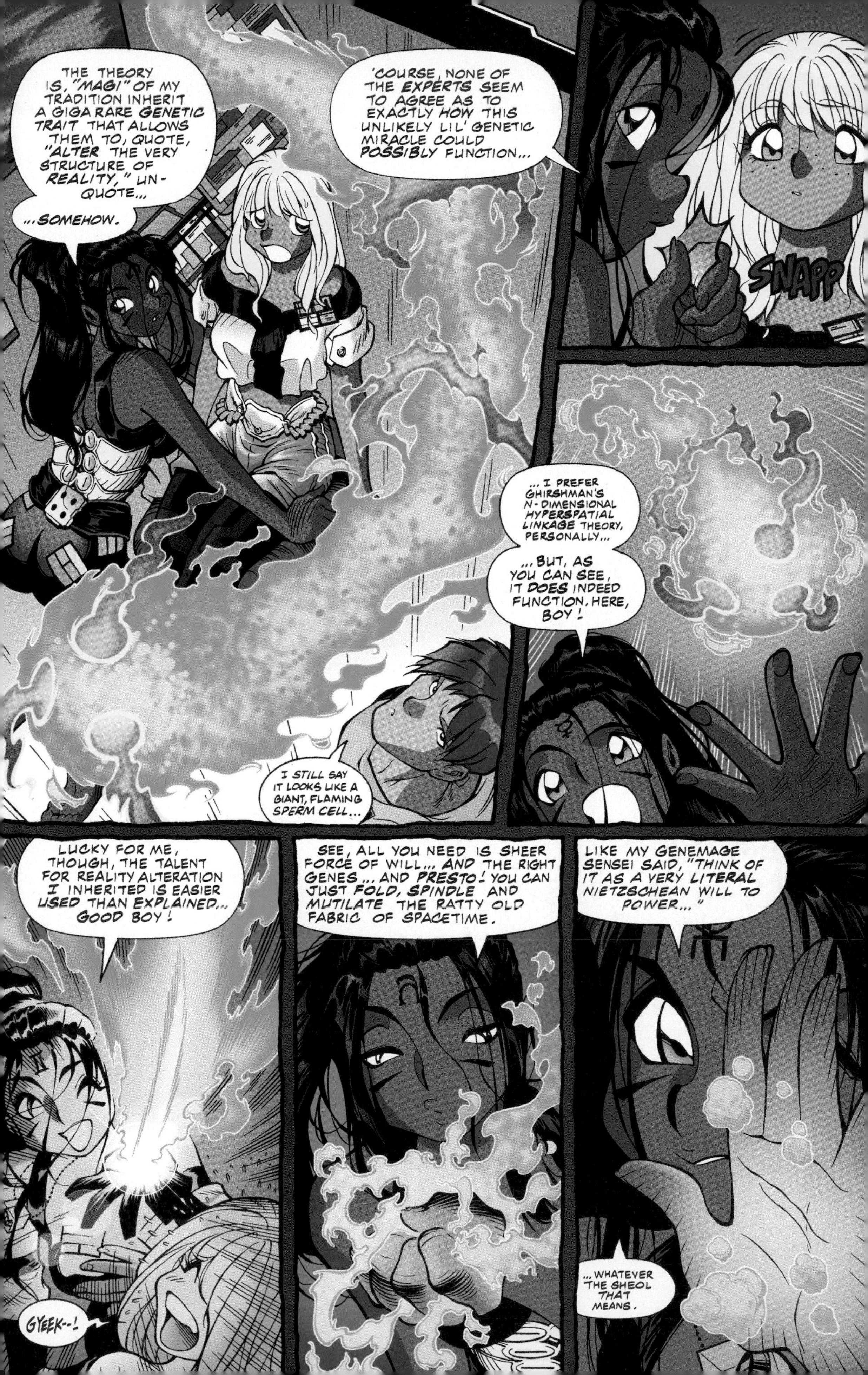
THE THEORY IS, "MAGI" OF MY TRADITION INHERIT A GIGA RARE GENETIC TRAIT THAT ALLOWS THEM TO, QUOTE, "ALTER THE VERY STRUCTURE OF REALITY," UN-QUOTE...
...SOMEHOW.
'COURSE, NONE OF THE EXPERTS SEEM TO AGREE AS TO EXACTLY HOW THIS UNLIKELY LIL' GENETIC MIRACLE COULD POSSIBLY FUNCTION...
SNAPP
...I PREFER GHIRSHMAN'S N-DIMENSIONAL HYPERSPATIAL LINKAGE THEORY, PERSONALLY...
...BUT, AS YOU CAN SEE, IT DOES INDEED FUNCTION. HERE, BOY!
I STILL SAY IT LOOKS LIKE A GIANT, FLAMING SPERM CELL...
LUCKY FOR ME, THOUGH, THE TALENT FOR REALITY ALTERATION I INHERITED IS EASIER USED THAN EXPLAINED... GOOD BOY!
GYEEK--!
SEE, ALL YOU NEED IS SHEER FORCE OF WILL... AND THE RIGHT GENES... AND PRESTO! YOU CAN JUST FOLD, SPINDLE AND MUTILATE THE RATTY OLD FABRIC OF SPACETIME.
LIKE MY GENEMAGE SENSEI SAID, "THINK OF IT AS A VERY LITERAL NIETZSCHEAN WILL TO POWER..."
...WHATEVER THE SHEOL THAT MEANS.

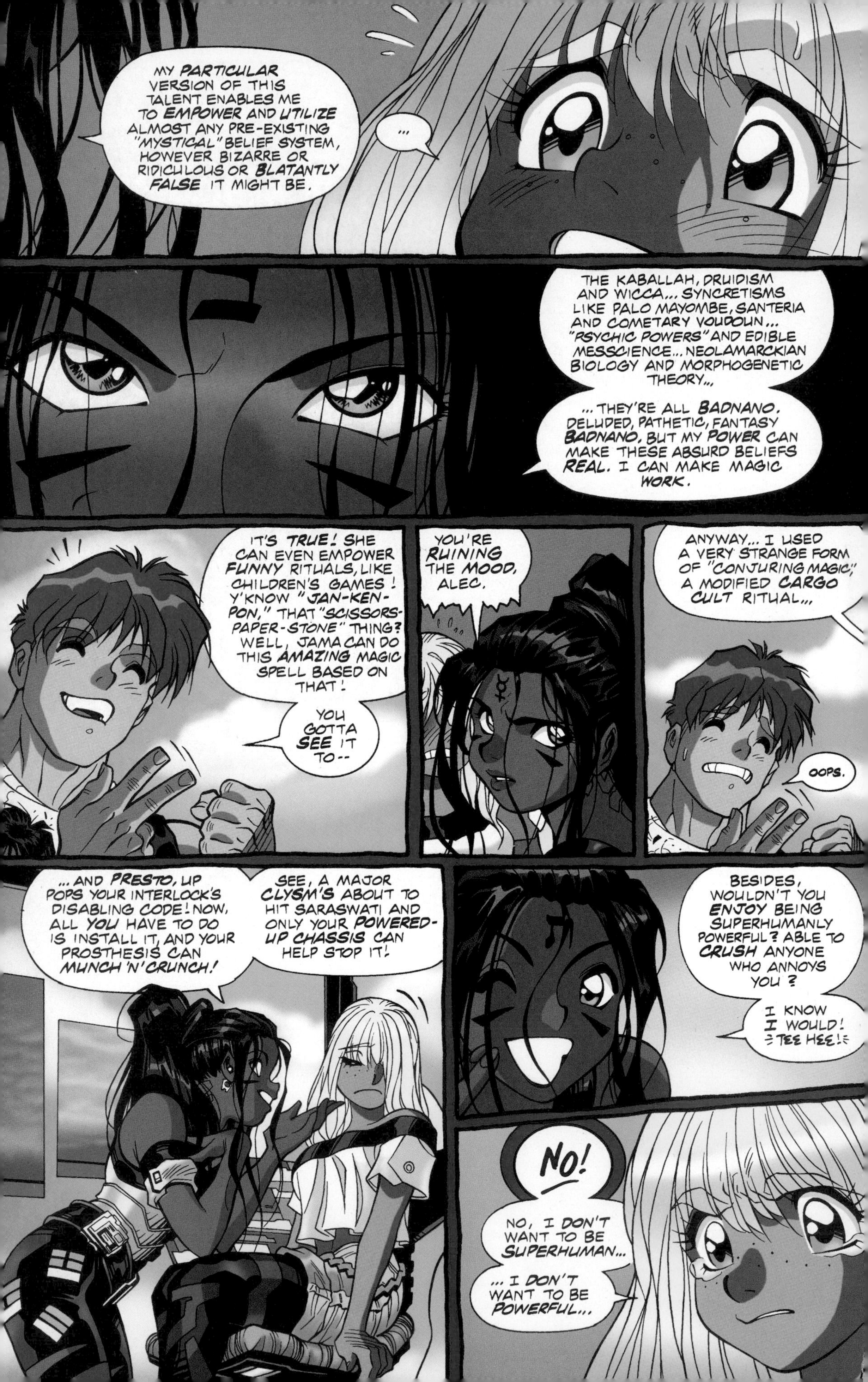

MY PARTICULAR VERSION OF THIS TALENT ENABLES ME TO EMPOWER AND UTILIZE ALMOST ANY PRE-EXISTING "MYSTICAL" BELIEF SYSTEM, HOWEVER BIZARRE OR RIDICULOUS OR BLATANTLY FALSE IT MIGHT BE.
...
THE KABALLAH, DRUIDISM AND WICCA... SYNCRETISMS LIKE PALO MAYOMBE, SANTERIA AND COMETARY VOUDOUN... "PSYCHIC POWERS" AND EDIBLE MESSCIENCE... NEOLAMARCKIAN BIOLOGY AND MORPHOGENETIC THEORY...
... THEY'RE ALL BADNANO. DELUDED, PATHETIC, FANTASY BADNANO. BUT MY POWER CAN MAKE THESE ABSURD BELIEFS REAL. I CAN MAKE MAGIC WORK.
IT'S TRUE! SHE CAN EVEN EMPOWER FUNNY RITUALS, LIKE CHILDREN'S GAMES! Y'KNOW "JAN-KEN-PON," THAT "SCISSORS-PAPER-STONE" THING? WELL, JAMA CAN DO THIS AMAZING MAGIC SPELL BASED ON THAT!
YOU GOTTA SEE IT TO--
YOU'RE RUINING THE MOOD, ALEC.
ANYWAY... I USED A VERY STRANGE FORM OF "CONJURING MAGIC," A MODIFIED CARGO CULT RITUAL...
OOPS.
... AND PRESTO, UP POPS YOUR INTERLOCK'S DISABLING CODE! NOW, ALL YOU HAVE TO DO IS INSTALL IT, AND YOUR PROSTHESIS CAN MUNCH 'N' CRUNCH!
SEE, A MAJOR CLYSM'S ABOUT TO HIT SARASWATI AND ONLY YOUR POWERED-UP CHASSIS CAN HELP STOP IT!
BESIDES, WOULDN'T YOU ENJOY BEING SUPERHUMANLY POWERFUL? ABLE TO CRUSH ANYONE WHO ANNOYS YOU?
I KNOW I WOULD! TEE HEE!
NO!
NO, I DON'T WANT TO BE SUPERHUMAN...
... I DON'T WANT TO BE POWERFUL...

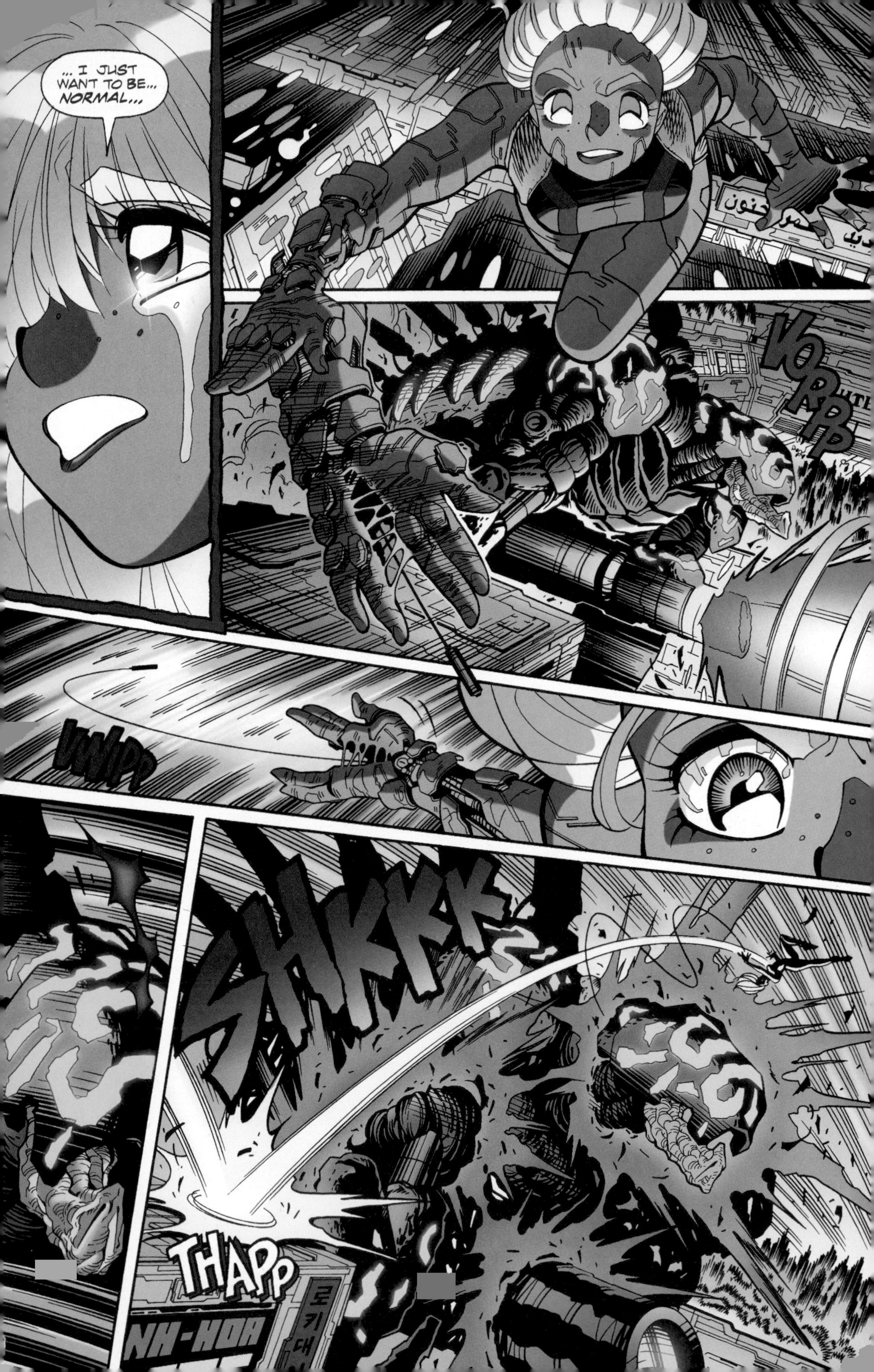
... I JUST WANT TO BE... NORMAL...
VORPP
SHKKK
THAPP
NH-HOA
로키대

SKRASH

WAYANG KULIT
CULTURAL RESOURCE CENTER

洋久

HUH?

SHHHH SHHHH SHHHH

SHHHH SHHHH

SHHH SHHHH

GABRIELLE..?

?

SHHHH

GHOD, IT IS GABRIELLE! WHAT'S HAPPENED TO HER...?

I DIDN'T KNOW SHE WAS A CYBORG! SHOCK, SHOCK!

N-NO....!

WAYANG KULIT
CULTURAL RESOURCE CEN

鶴田洋久

LOOK OUT!

RUN AWAY!

D-DON'T LOOK AT ME...

...PLEASE...

UH, GABRIELLE ...ARE YOU, UH, ALL RIGHT?

WHAT ARE THOSE CRACKS IN HER SKIN? MUY GROSS...

WAYANG KULIT

THMPP

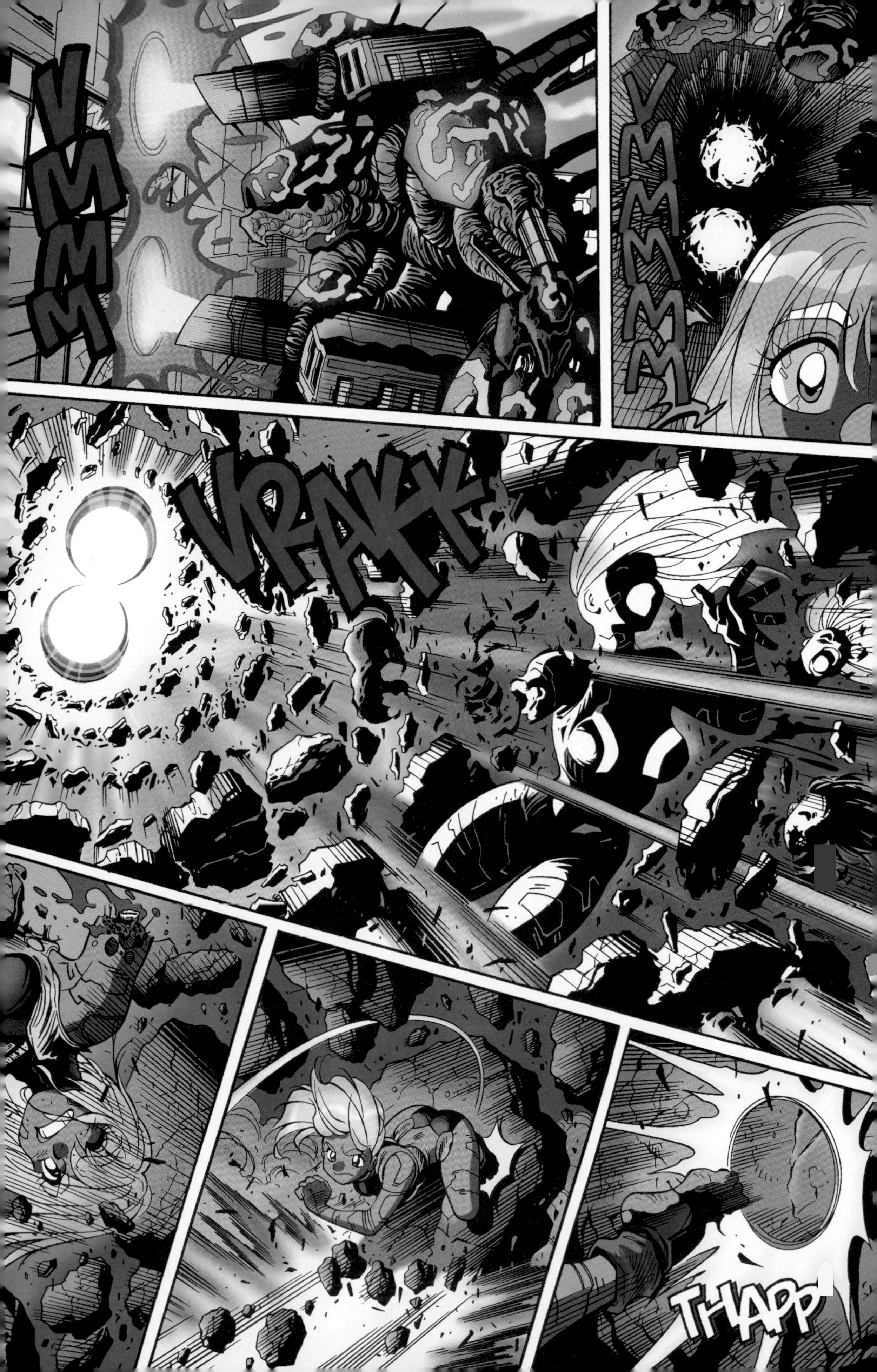
VMMM
VMMMMM
VRAKK
THAPP

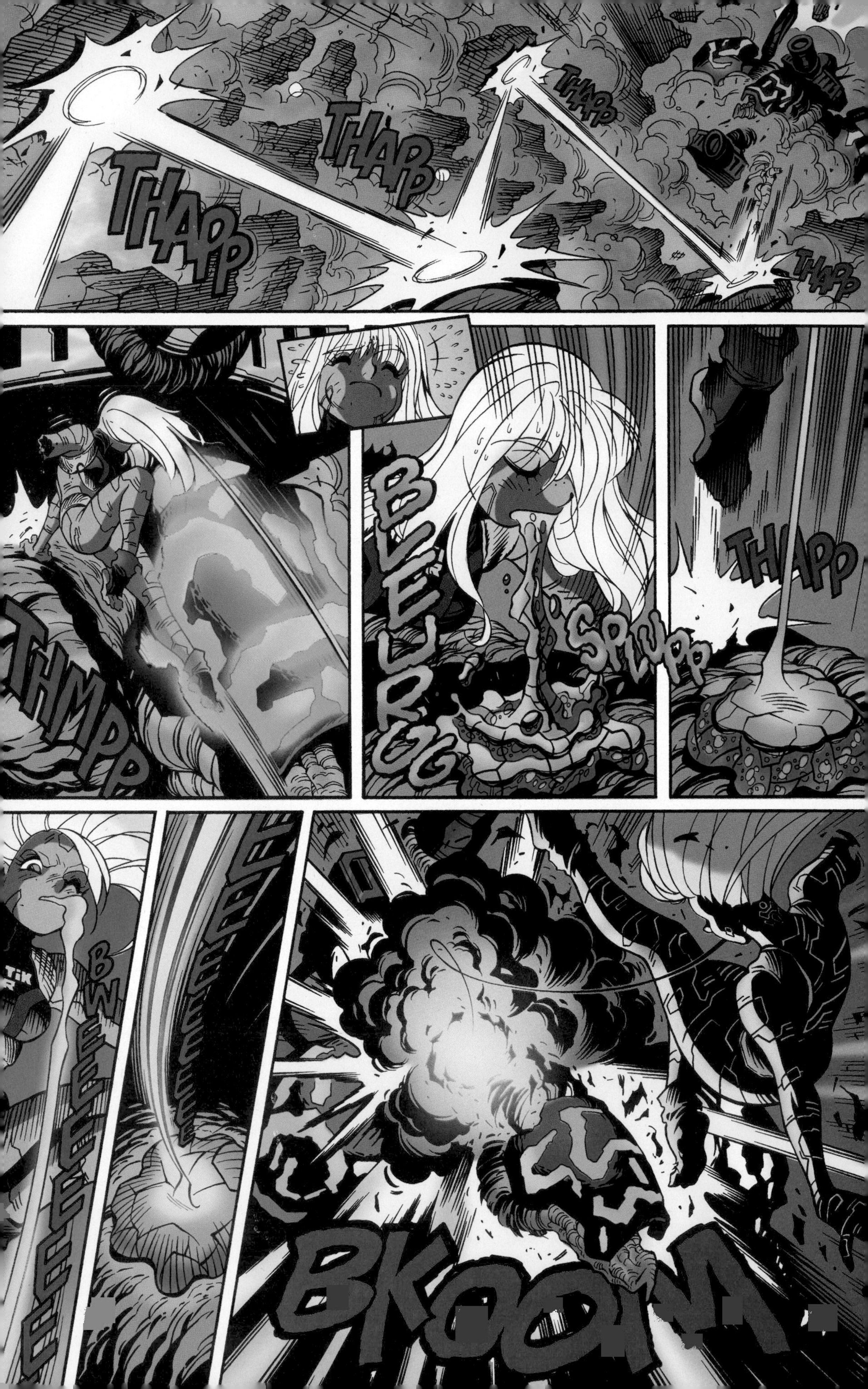
THAPP
THAPP
THAPP
THAPP
THMPP
BLEURGG
SPLUPP
THAPP
BWEEEEEEEEEE
EEEEEEEEEE
BKOOM

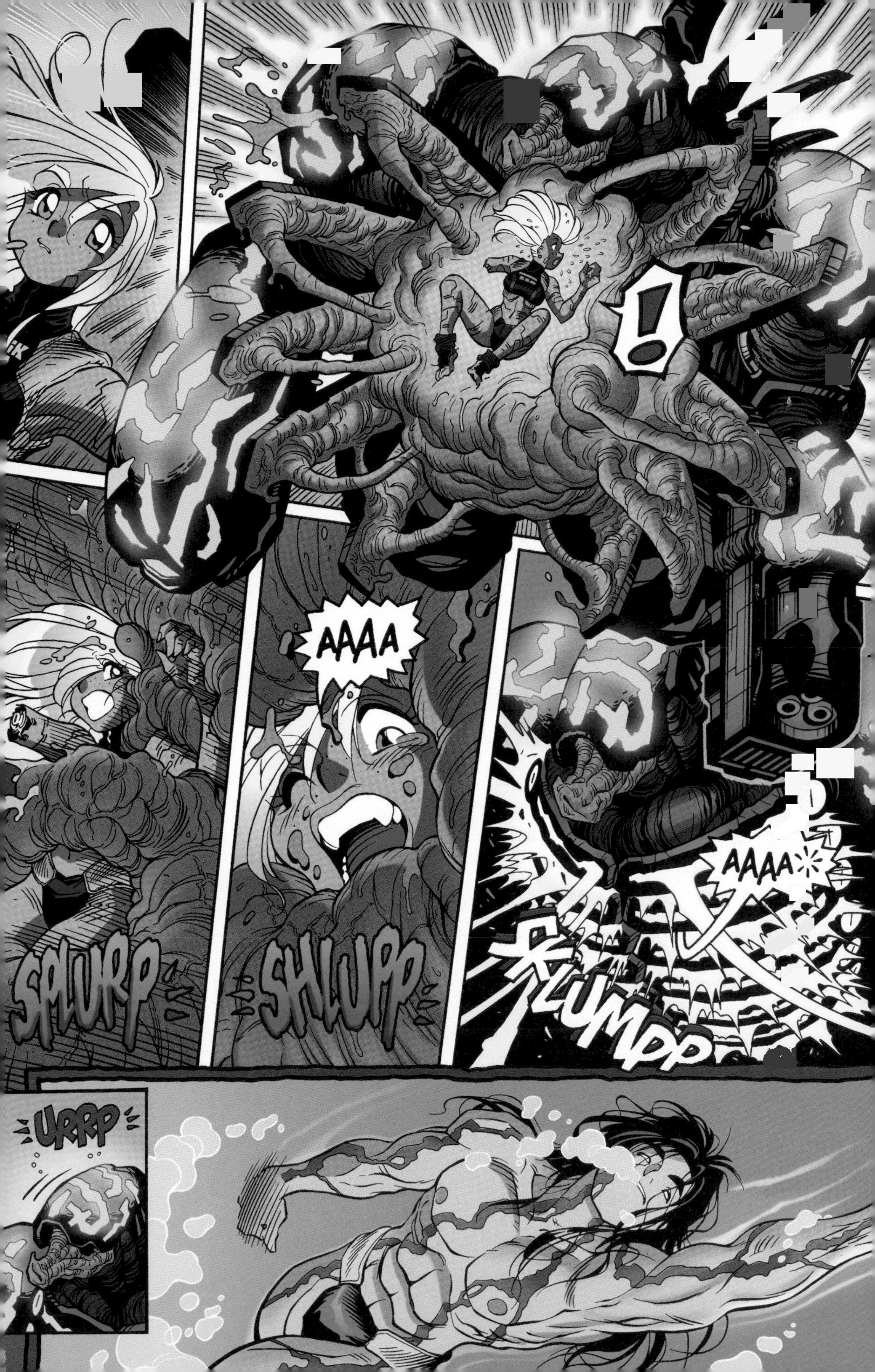
!
AAAA
AAAA
SPLURP
SHLUPP
SPLUMPP
URRP

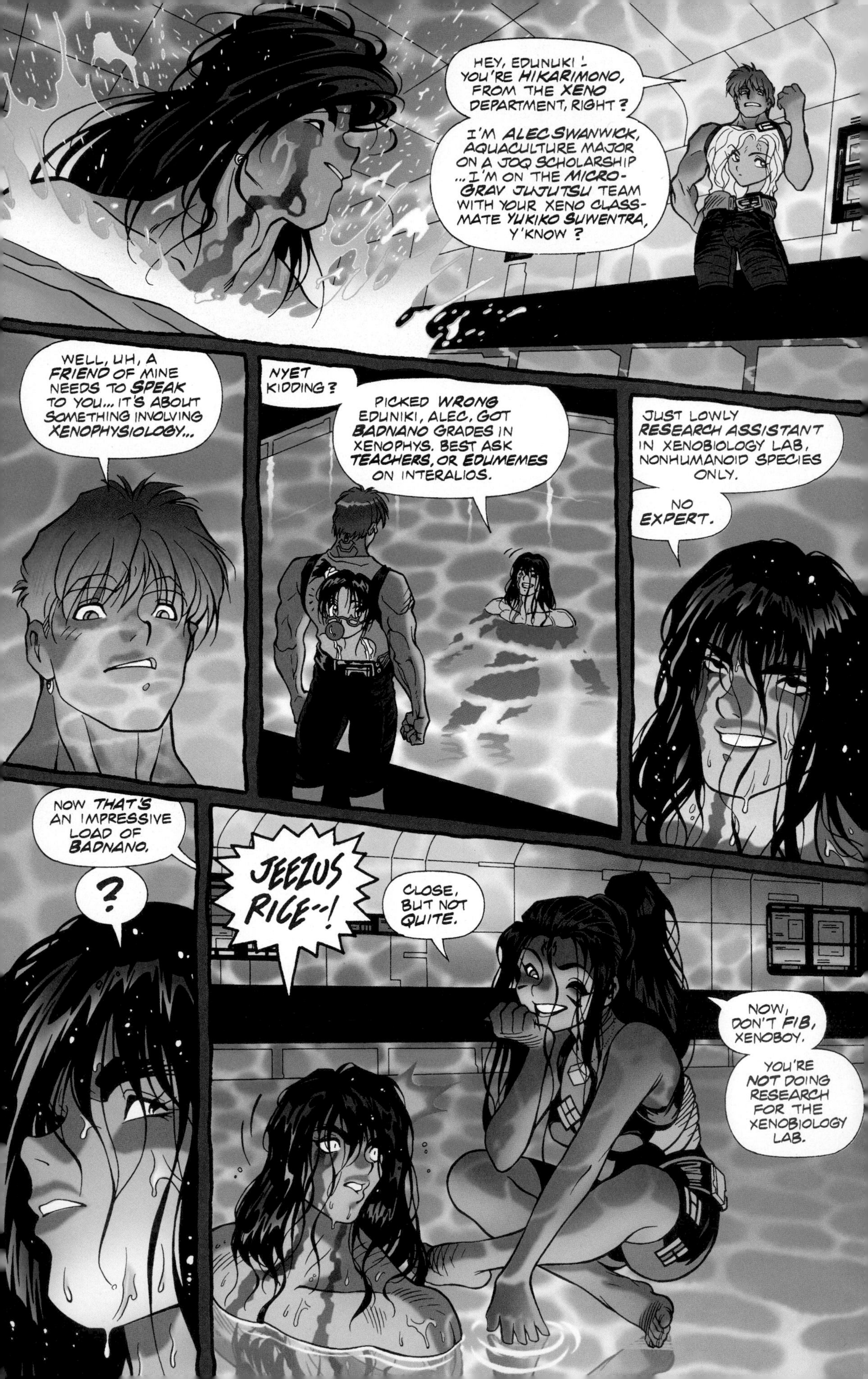
HEY, EDUNUKI! - YOU'RE HIKARIMONO, FROM THE XENO DEPARTMENT, RIGHT?
I'M ALEC SWANWICK, AQUACULTURE MAJOR ON A JOQ SCHOLARSHIP ...I'M ON THE MICRO-GRAV JUJUTSU TEAM WITH YOUR XENO CLASSMATE YUKIKO SUWENTRA, Y'KNOW?
WELL, UH, A FRIEND OF MINE NEEDS TO SPEAK TO YOU... IT'S ABOUT SOMETHING INVOLVING XENOPHYSIOLOGY...
NYET KIDDING?
PICKED WRONG EDUNIKI, ALEC. GOT BADNANO GRADES IN XENOPHYS. BEST ASK TEACHERS, OR EDUMEMES ON INTERALIOS.
JUST LOWLY RESEARCH ASSISTANT IN XENOBIOLOGY LAB, NONHUMANOID SPECIES ONLY.
NO EXPERT.
NOW THAT'S AN IMPRESSIVE LOAD OF BADNANO.
?
JEEZUS RICE--!
CLOSE, BUT NOT QUITE.
NOW, DON'T FIB, XENOBOY.
YOU'RE NOT DOING RESEARCH FOR THE XENOBIOLOGY LAB.

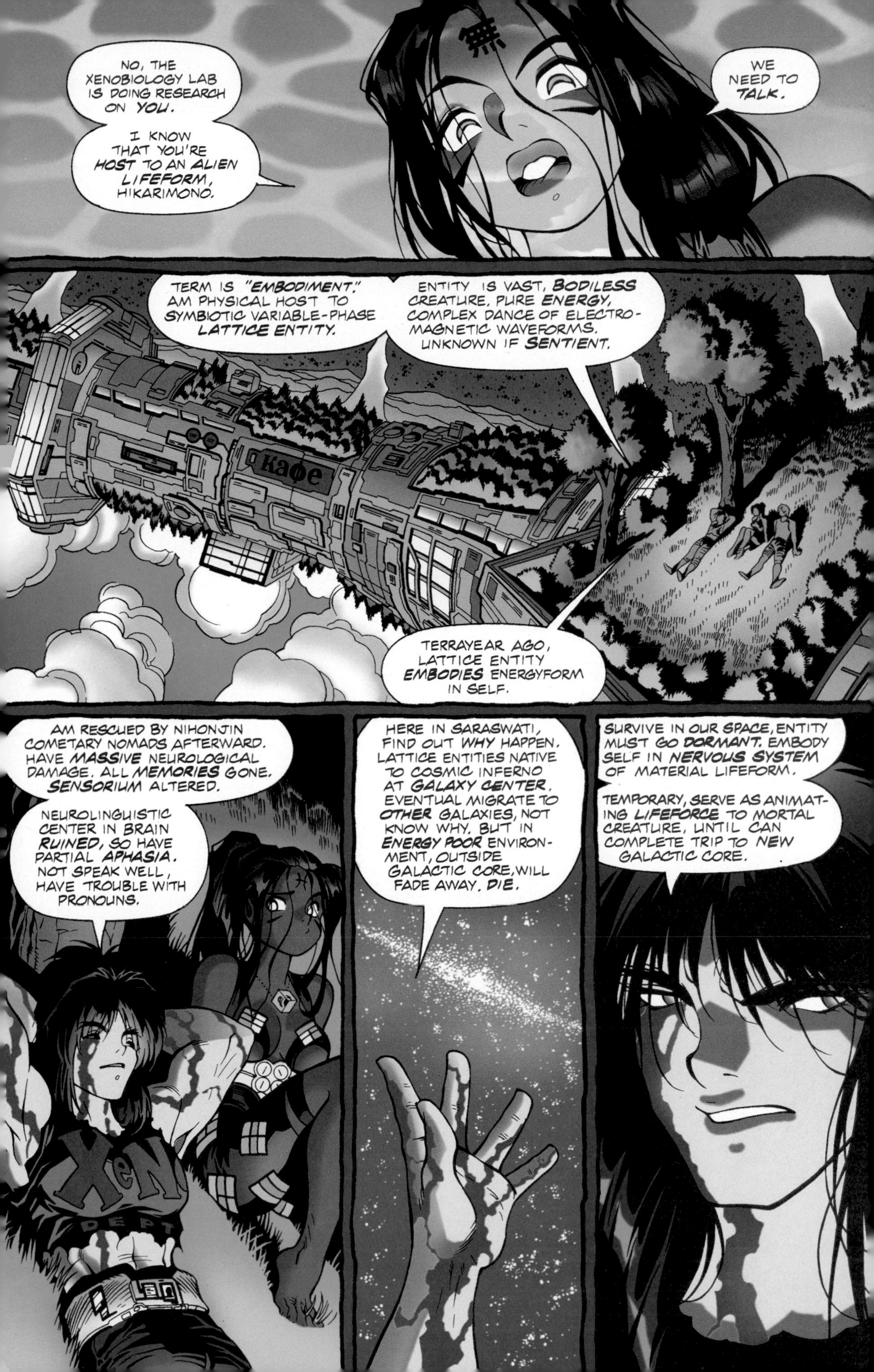

NO, THE XENOBIOLOGY LAB IS DOING RESEARCH ON *YOU*.
I KNOW THAT YOU'RE *HOST* TO AN *ALIEN LIFEFORM*, HIKARIMONO.
WE NEED TO *TALK*.
TERM IS *"EMBODIMENT."* AM PHYSICAL HOST TO SYMBIOTIC VARIABLE-PHASE *LATTICE ENTITY*.
ENTITY IS VAST, *BODILESS* CREATURE. PURE *ENERGY*, COMPLEX DANCE OF ELECTRO-MAGNETIC WAVEFORMS. UNKNOWN IF *SENTIENT*.
Кафе
TERRAYEAR AGO, LATTICE ENTITY *EMBODIES* ENERGYFORM IN SELF.
AM RESCUED BY NIHONJIN COMETARY NOMADS AFTERWARD. HAVE *MASSIVE* NEUROLOGICAL DAMAGE. ALL *MEMORIES* GONE. *SENSORIUM* ALTERED.
NEUROLINGUISTIC CENTER IN BRAIN *RUINED*, SO HAVE PARTIAL *APHASIA*. NOT SPEAK WELL, HAVE TROUBLE WITH PRONOUNS.
HERE IN SARASWATI, FIND OUT *WHY* HAPPEN. LATTICE ENTITIES NATIVE TO COSMIC INFERNO AT *GALAXY CENTER*, EVENTUAL MIGRATE TO *OTHER* GALAXIES, NOT KNOW WHY. BUT IN *ENERGY POOR* ENVIRONMENT, OUTSIDE GALACTIC CORE, WILL FADE AWAY, *DIE*.
SURVIVE IN OUR SPACE, ENTITY MUST GO *DORMANT*. EMBODY SELF IN *NERVOUS SYSTEM* OF MATERIAL LIFEFORM.
TEMPORARY, SERVE AS ANIMATING *LIFEFORCE* TO MORTAL CREATURE, UNTIL CAN COMPLETE TRIP TO *NEW* GALACTIC CORE.

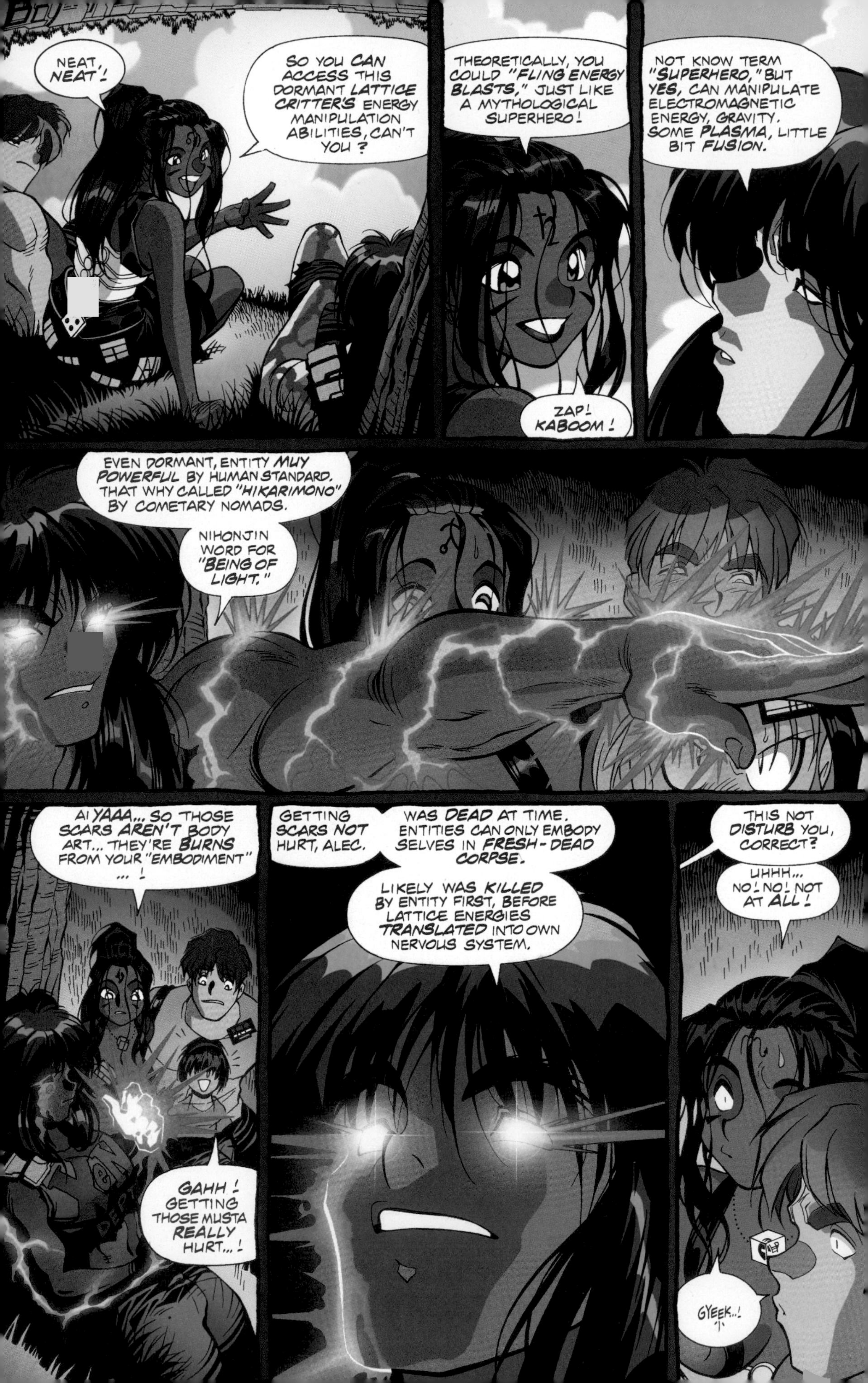
NEAT, NEAT!
SO YOU CAN ACCESS THIS DORMANT LATTICE CRITTER'S ENERGY MANIPULATION ABILITIES, CAN'T YOU?
THEORETICALLY, YOU COULD "FLING ENERGY BLASTS," JUST LIKE A MYTHOLOGICAL SUPERHERO!
ZAP! KABOOM!
NOT KNOW TERM "SUPERHERO," BUT YES, CAN MANIPULATE ELECTROMAGNETIC ENERGY, GRAVITY. SOME PLASMA, LITTLE BIT FUSION.
EVEN DORMANT, ENTITY MUY POWERFUL BY HUMAN STANDARD. THAT WHY CALLED "HIKARIMONO" BY COMETARY NOMADS.
NIHONJIN WORD FOR "BEING OF LIGHT."
AI YAAA... SO THOSE SCARS AREN'T BODY ART... THEY'RE BURNS FROM YOUR "EMBODIMENT" ...!
GAHH! GETTING THOSE MUSTA REALLY HURT...!
GETTING SCARS NOT HURT, ALEC.
WAS DEAD AT TIME. ENTITIES CAN ONLY EMBODY SELVES IN FRESH-DEAD CORPSE.
LIKELY WAS KILLED BY ENTITY FIRST, BEFORE LATTICE ENERGIES TRANSLATED INTO OWN NERVOUS SYSTEM.
THIS NOT DISTURB YOU, CORRECT?
UHHH... NO! NO! NOT AT ALL!
GYEEK..!

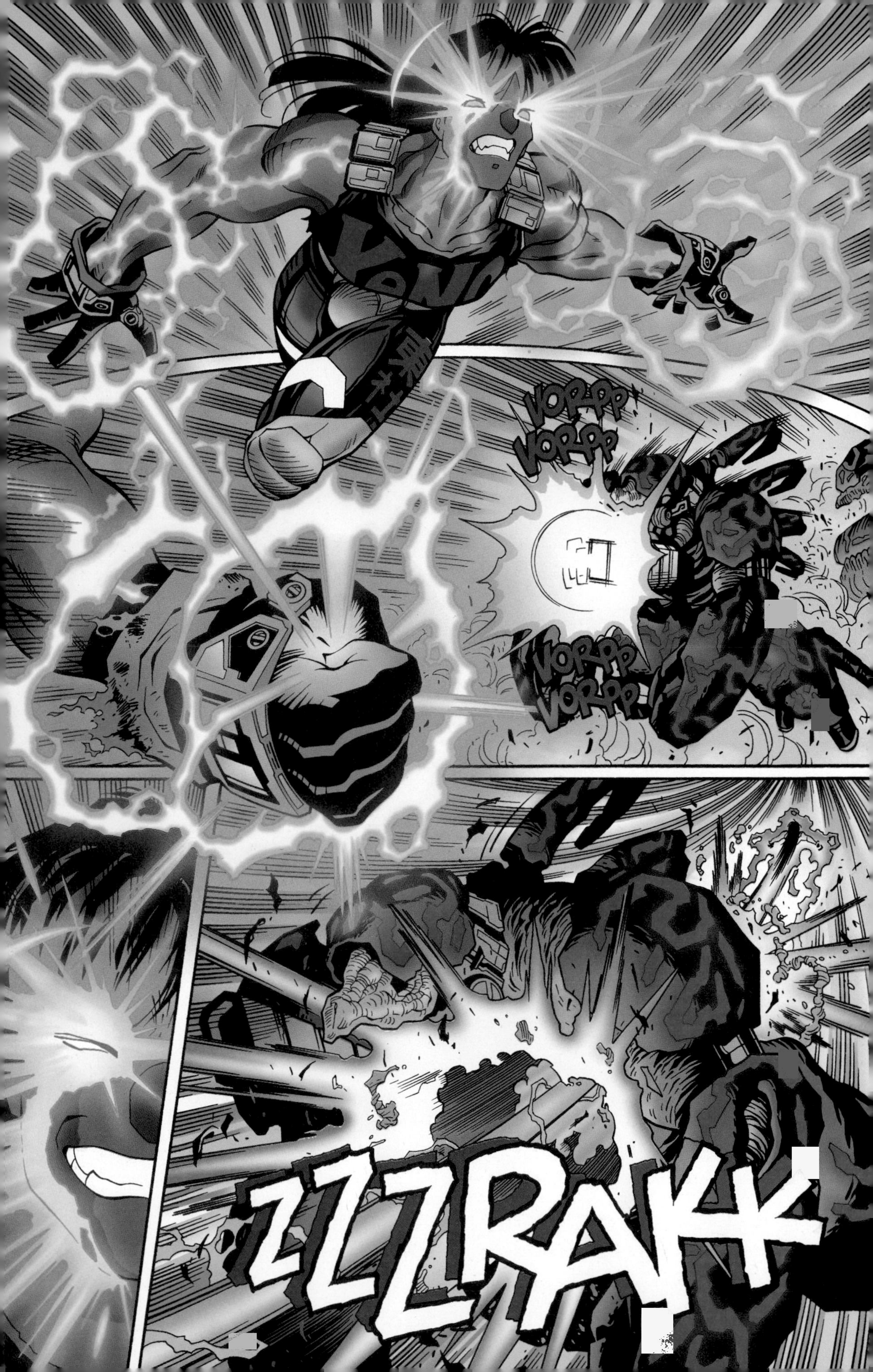
VORPP
VORPP
VORPP
VORPP
ZZZRAK!

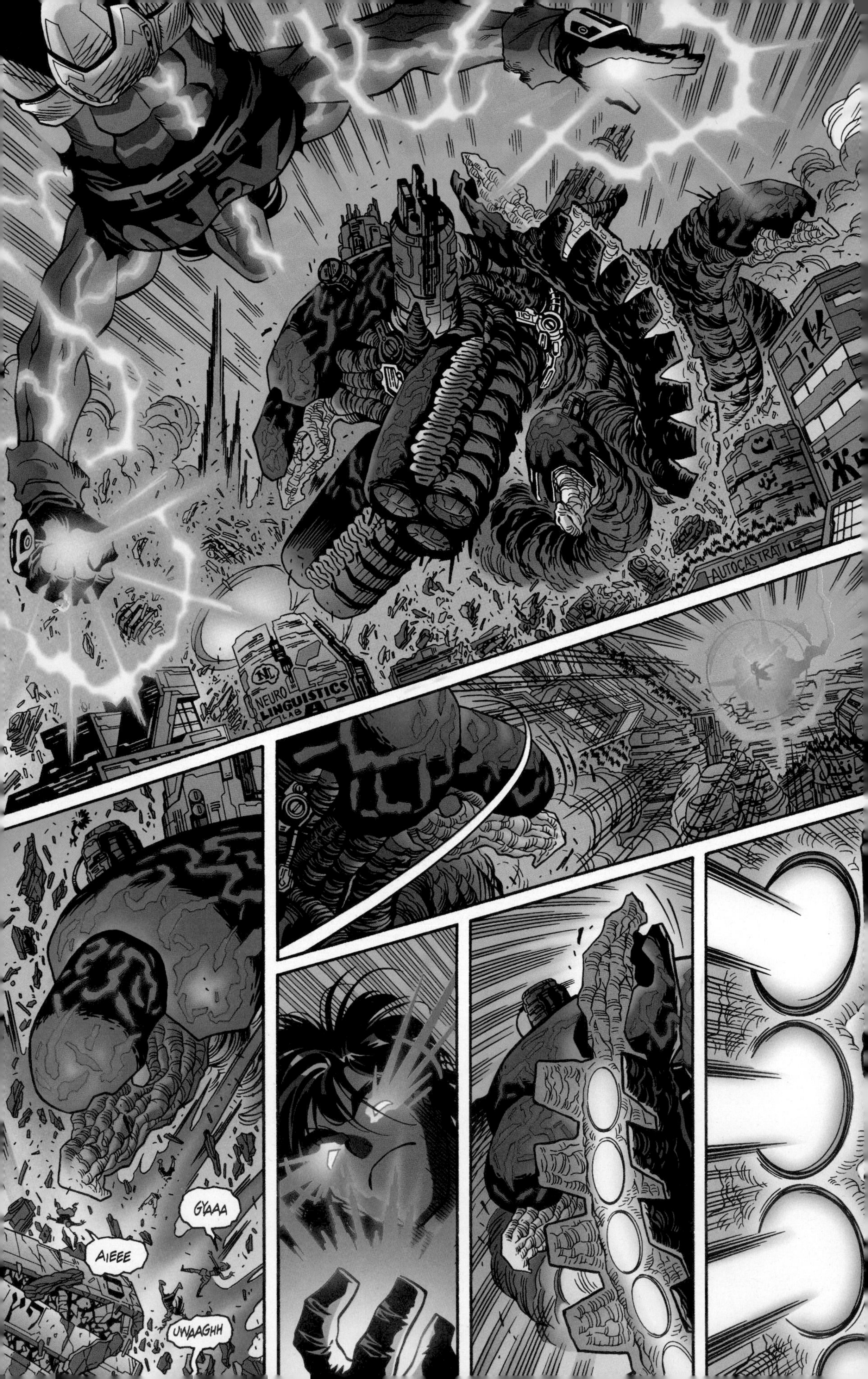
AUTOCASTRATI
NEURO
LINGUISTICS
LAB
GYAAA
AIEEE
UWAAGHH

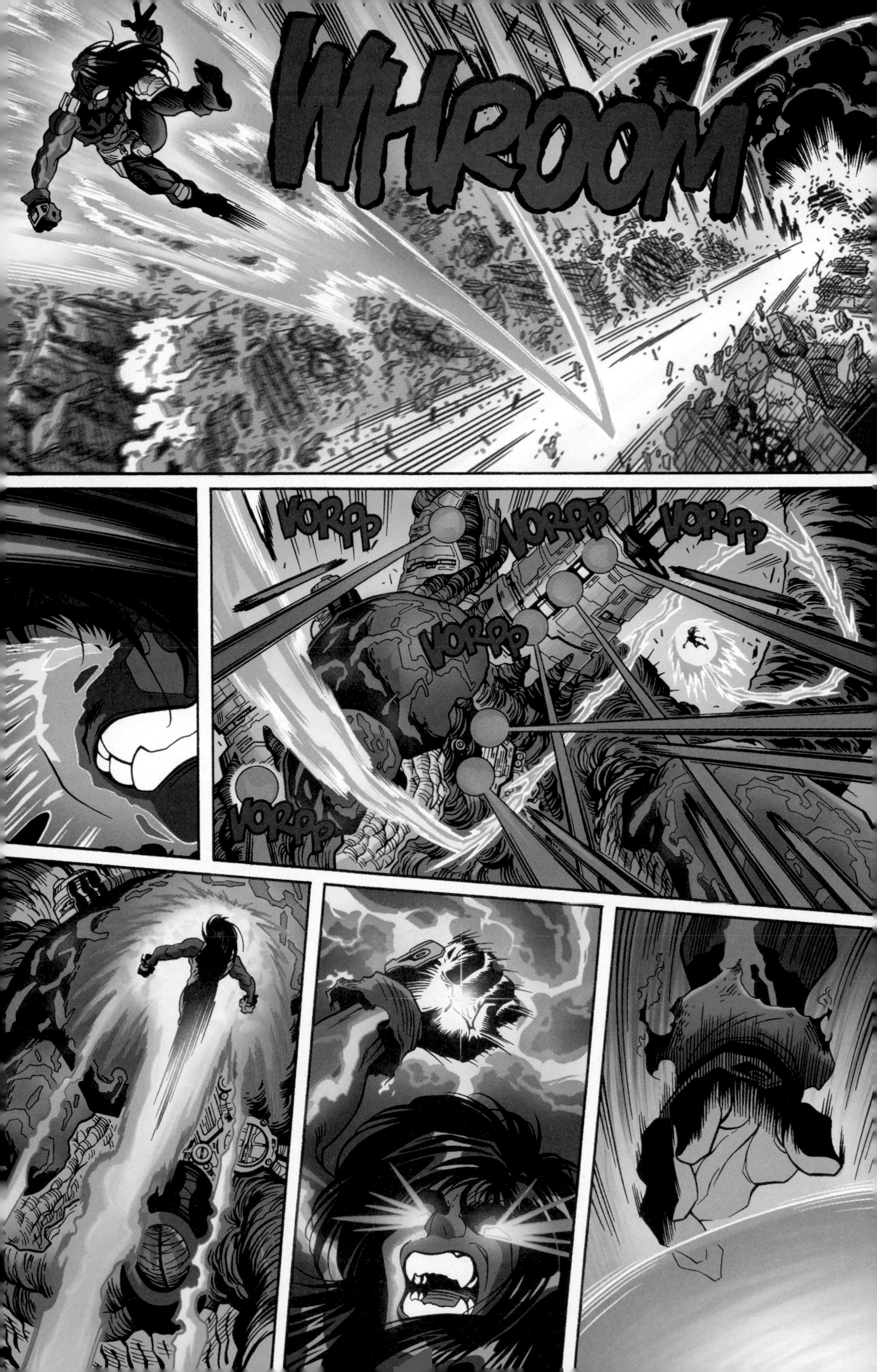
WHROOM
VORPP
VORPP
VORPP
VORPP
VORPP

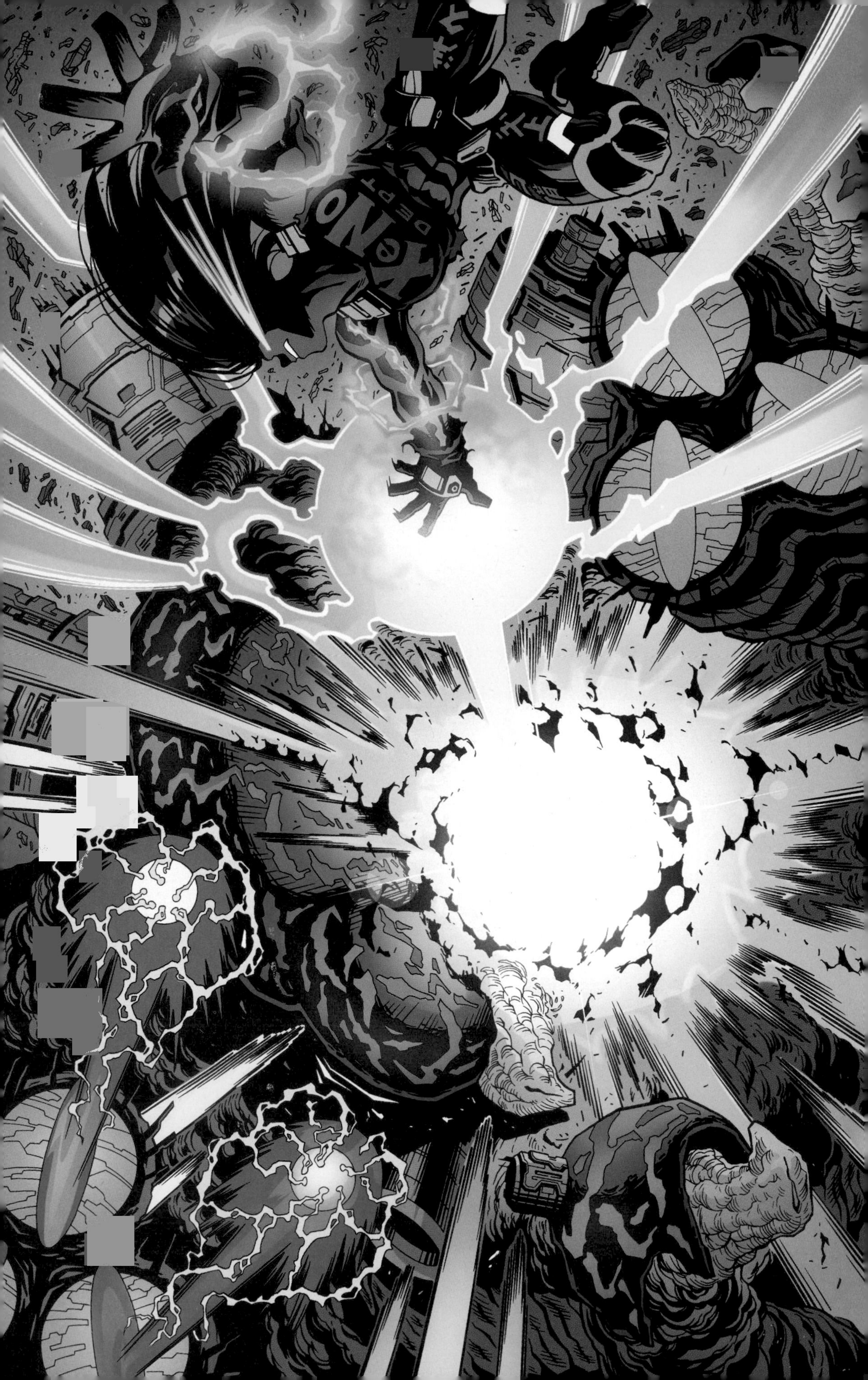

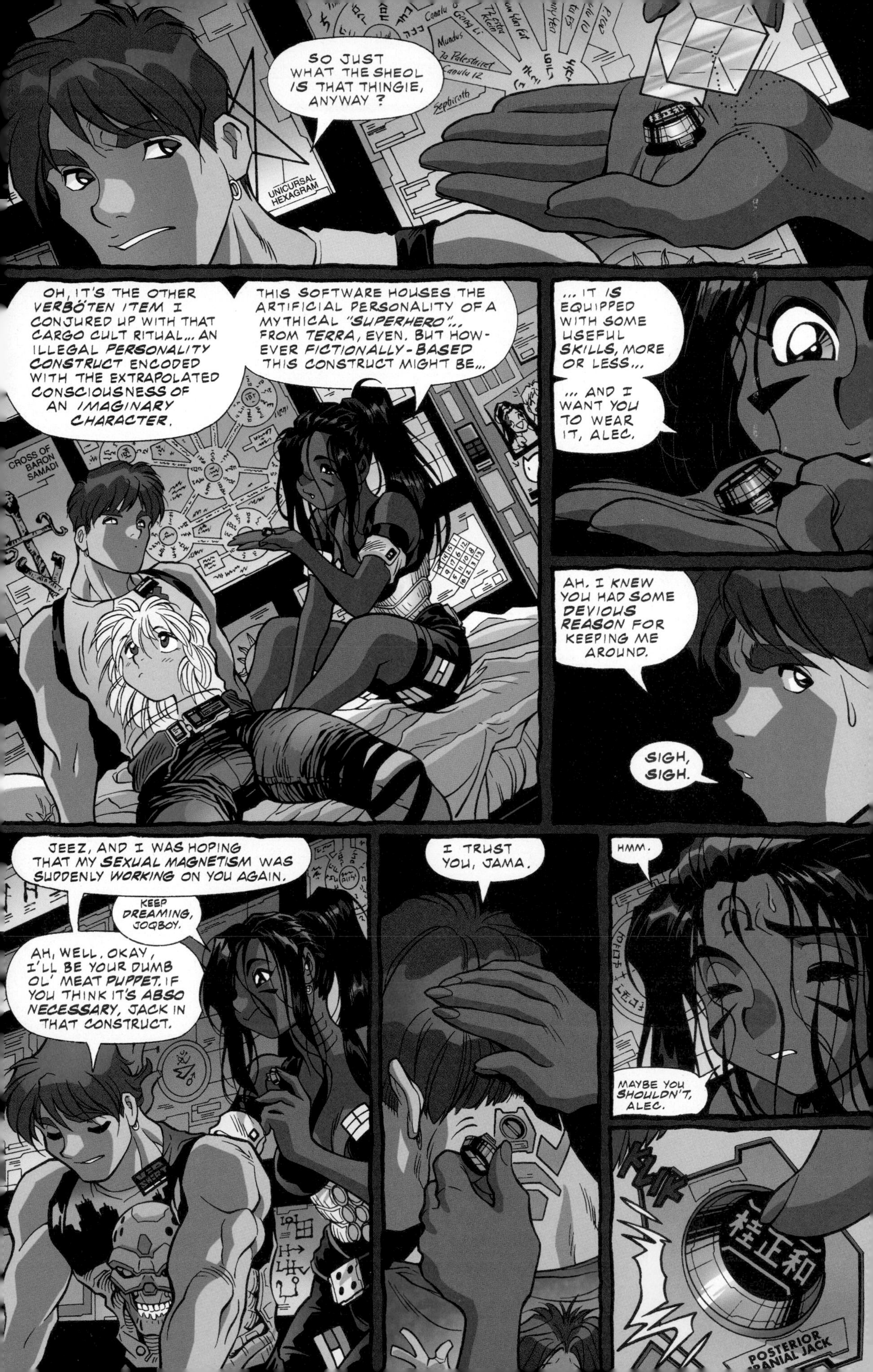
SO JUST WHAT THE SHEOL IS THAT THINGIE, ANYWAY?
UNICURSAL HEXAGRAM
OH, IT'S THE OTHER VERBÖTEN ITEM I CONJURED UP WITH THAT CARGO CULT RITUAL... AN ILLEGAL PERSONALITY CONSTRUCT ENCODED WITH THE EXTRAPOLATED CONSCIOUSNESS OF AN IMAGINARY CHARACTER.
THIS SOFTWARE HOUSES THE ARTIFICIAL PERSONALITY OF A MYTHICAL "SUPERHERO"... FROM TERRA, EVEN. BUT HOWEVER FICTIONALLY-BASED THIS CONSTRUCT MIGHT BE...
CROSS OF BARON SAMADI
... IT IS EQUIPPED WITH SOME USEFUL SKILLS, MORE OR LESS...
... AND I WANT YOU TO WEAR IT, ALEC.
AH. I KNEW YOU HAD SOME DEVIOUS REASON FOR KEEPING ME AROUND.
SIGH, SIGH.
JEEZ, AND I WAS HOPING THAT MY SEXUAL MAGNETISM WAS SUDDENLY WORKING ON YOU AGAIN.
KEEP DREAMING, JOQBOY.
AH, WELL, OKAY, I'LL BE YOUR DUMB OL' MEAT PUPPET. IF YOU THINK IT'S ABSO NECESSARY, JACK IN THAT CONSTRUCT.
I TRUST YOU, JAMA.
HMM.
MAYBE YOU SHOULDN'T, ALEC.
KLIK
POSTERIOR CRANIAL JACK

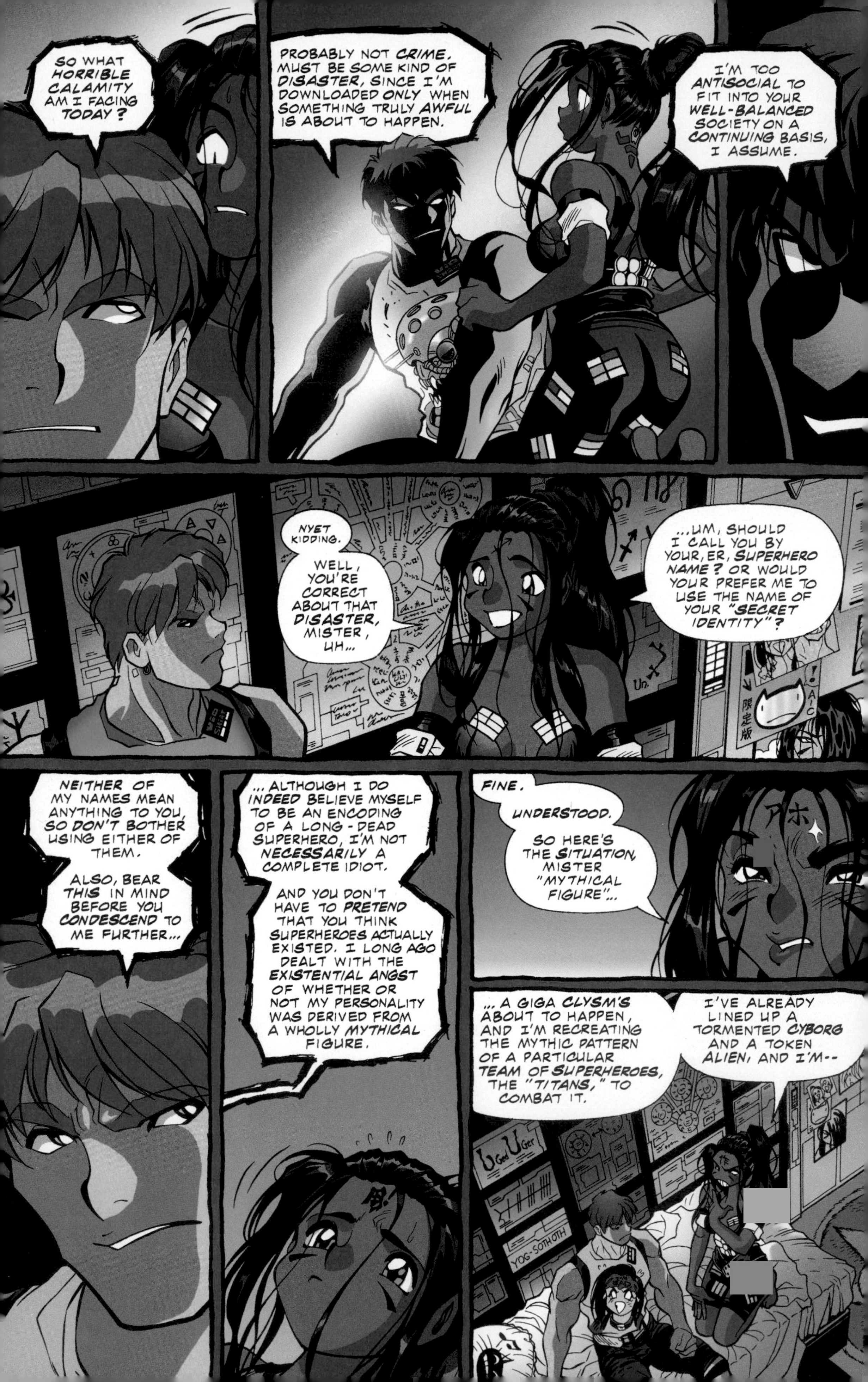
SO WHAT HORRIBLE CALAMITY AM I FACING TODAY?
PROBABLY NOT CRIME. MUST BE SOME KIND OF DISASTER, SINCE I'M DOWNLOADED ONLY WHEN SOMETHING TRULY AWFUL IS ABOUT TO HAPPEN.
I'M TOO ANTISOCIAL TO FIT INTO YOUR WELL-BALANCED SOCIETY ON A CONTINUING BASIS, I ASSUME.
NYET KIDDING.
WELL, YOU'RE CORRECT ABOUT THAT DISASTER, MISTER, UH...
...UM, SHOULD I CALL YOU BY YOUR, ER, SUPERHERO NAME? OR WOULD YOUR PREFER ME TO USE THE NAME OF YOUR "SECRET IDENTITY"?
NEITHER OF MY NAMES MEAN ANYTHING TO YOU, SO DON'T BOTHER USING EITHER OF THEM.
ALSO, BEAR THIS IN MIND BEFORE YOU CONDESCEND TO ME FURTHER...
...ALTHOUGH I DO INDEED BELIEVE MYSELF TO BE AN ENCODING OF A LONG-DEAD SUPERHERO, I'M NOT NECESSARILY A COMPLETE IDIOT.
AND YOU DON'T HAVE TO PRETEND THAT YOU THINK SUPERHEROES ACTUALLY EXISTED. I LONG AGO DEALT WITH THE EXISTENTIAL ANGST OF WHETHER OR NOT MY PERSONALITY WAS DERIVED FROM A WHOLLY MYTHICAL FIGURE.
FINE.
UNDERSTOOD.
SO HERE'S THE SITUATION, MISTER "MYTHICAL FIGURE"...
...A GIGA CLYSM'S ABOUT TO HAPPEN, AND I'M RECREATING THE MYTHIC PATTERN OF A PARTICULAR TEAM OF SUPERHEROES, THE "TITANS," TO COMBAT IT.
I'VE ALREADY LINED UP A TORMENTED CYBORG AND A TOKEN ALIEN, AND I'M--
YOG-SOTHOTH

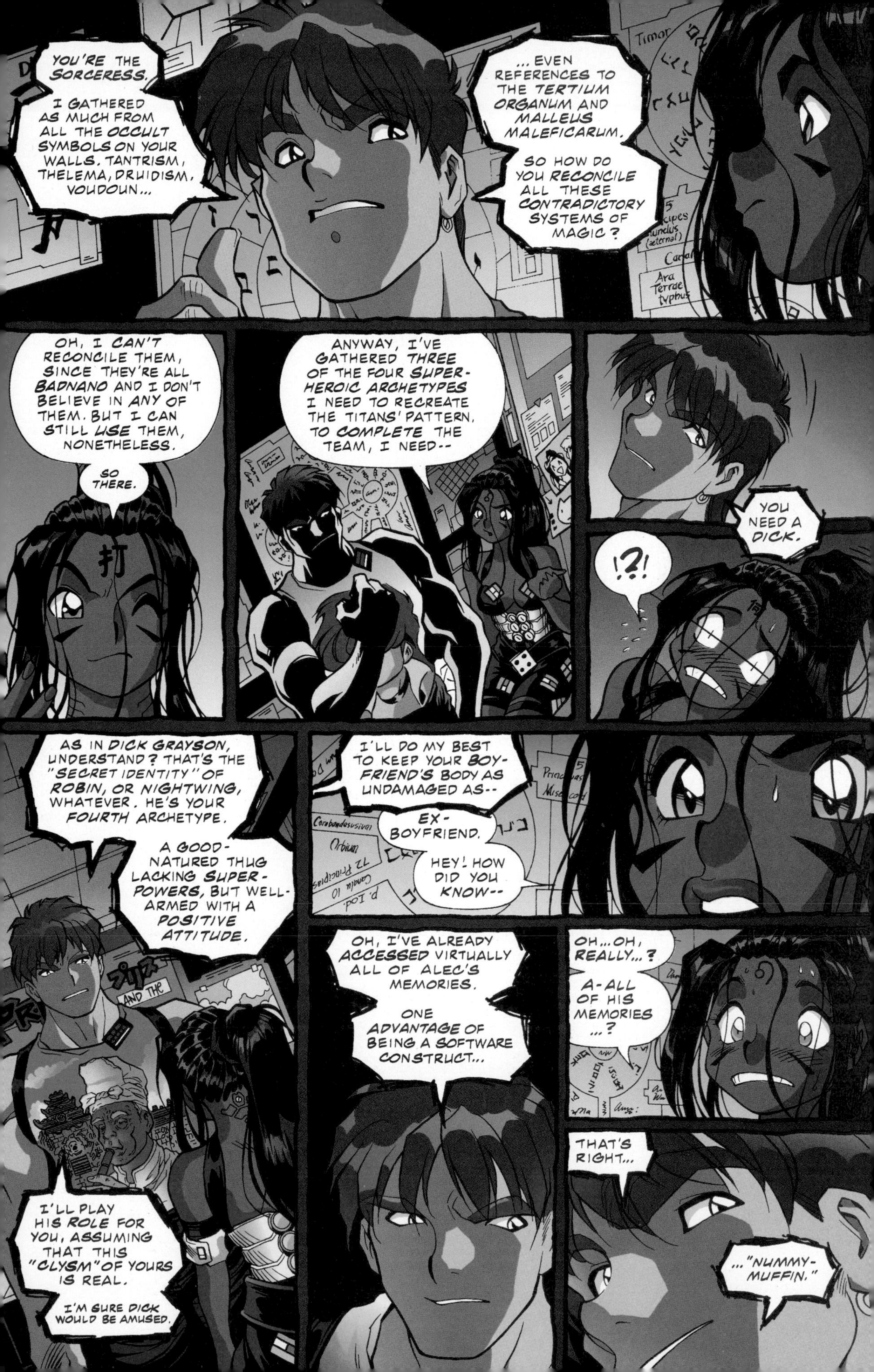

YOU'RE THE SORCERESS.
I GATHERED AS MUCH FROM ALL THE OCCULT SYMBOLS ON YOUR WALLS. TANTRISM, THELEMA, DRUIDISM, VOUDOUN...
... EVEN REFERENCES TO THE TERTIUM ORGANUM AND MALLEUS MALEFICARUM.
SO HOW DO YOU RECONCILE ALL THESE CONTRADICTORY SYSTEMS OF MAGIC?
OH, I CAN'T RECONCILE THEM, SINCE THEY'RE ALL BADNANO AND I DON'T BELIEVE IN ANY OF THEM. BUT I CAN STILL USE THEM, NONETHELESS.
SO THERE.
ANYWAY, I'VE GATHERED THREE OF THE FOUR SUPER-HEROIC ARCHETYPES I NEED TO RECREATE THE TITANS' PATTERN. TO COMPLETE THE TEAM, I NEED--
YOU NEED A DICK.
!?!
AS IN DICK GRAYSON, UNDERSTAND? THAT'S THE "SECRET IDENTITY" OF ROBIN, OR NIGHTWING, WHATEVER. HE'S YOUR FOURTH ARCHETYPE.
A GOOD-NATURED THUG LACKING SUPER-POWERS, BUT WELL-ARMED WITH A POSITIVE ATTITUDE.
I'LL PLAY HIS ROLE FOR YOU, ASSUMING THAT THIS "CLYSM" OF YOURS IS REAL.
I'M SURE DICK WOULD BE AMUSED.
I'LL DO MY BEST TO KEEP YOUR BOY-FRIEND'S BODY AS UNDAMAGED AS--
EX-BOYFRIEND.
HEY! HOW DID YOU KNOW--
OH, I'VE ALREADY ACCESSED VIRTUALLY ALL OF ALEC'S MEMORIES.
ONE ADVANTAGE OF BEING A SOFTWARE CONSTRUCT...
OH...OH, REALLY...?
A-ALL OF HIS MEMORIES ...?
THAT'S RIGHT...
..."NUMMY-MUFFIN."

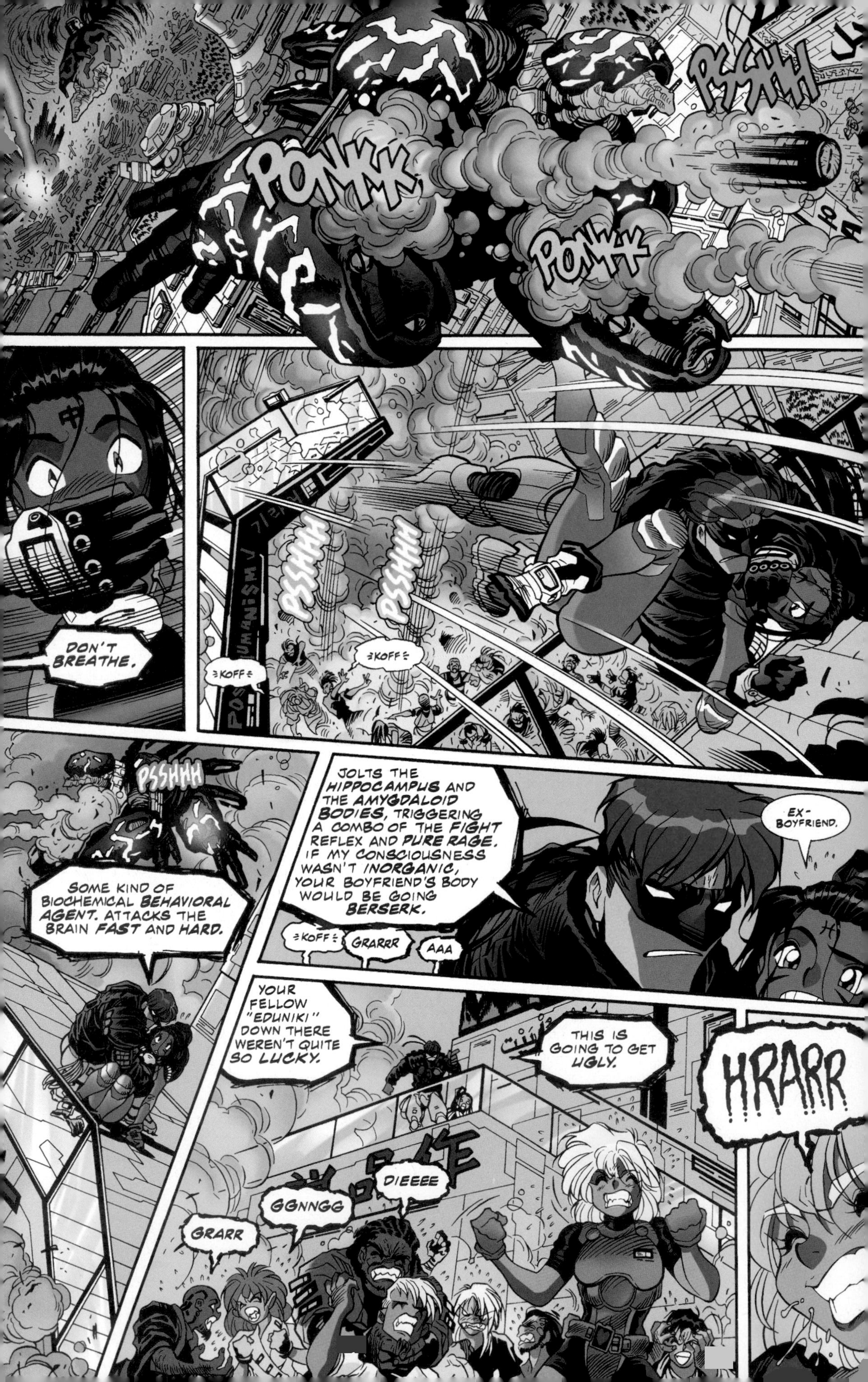
PSSHH
PONKK
PONKK
DON'T BREATHE.
KOFF
KOFF
PSSHHH
PSSHHH
PSSHHH
SOME KIND OF BIOCHEMICAL BEHAVIORAL AGENT. ATTACKS THE BRAIN FAST AND HARD.
JOLTS THE HIPPOCAMPUS AND THE AMYGDALOID BODIES, TRIGGERING A COMBO OF THE FIGHT REFLEX AND PURE RAGE. IF MY CONSCIOUSNESS WASN'T INORGANIC, YOUR BOYFRIEND'S BODY WOULD BE GOING BERSERK.
KOFF
GRARRR
AAA
EX-BOYFRIEND.
YOUR FELLOW "EDUNIKI" DOWN THERE WEREN'T QUITE SO LUCKY.
THIS IS GOING TO GET UGLY.
HRARR
DIEEEE
GGNNGG
GRARR

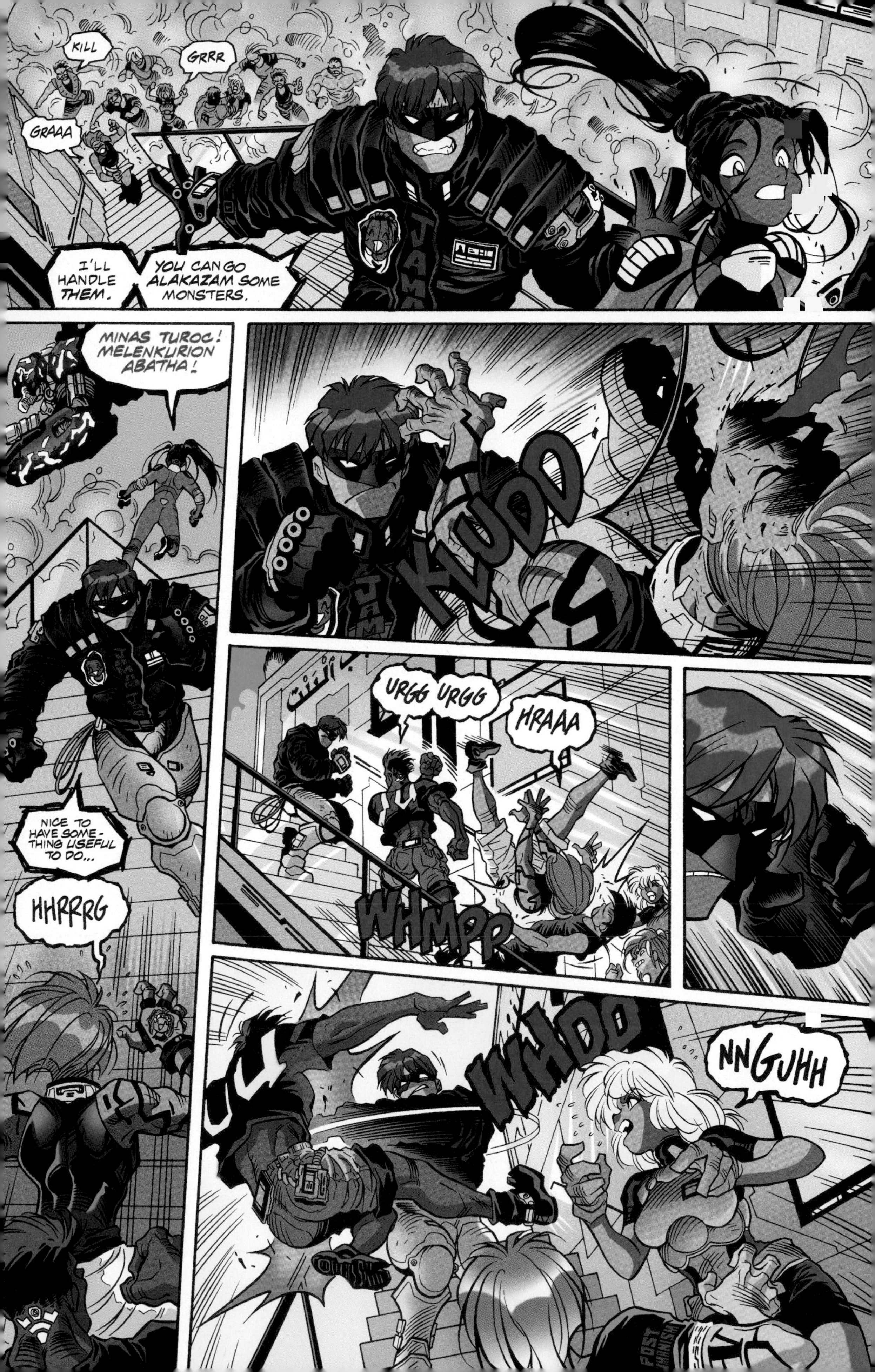

KILL
GRRR
GRAAA
I'LL HANDLE THEM.
YOU CAN GO ALAKAZAM SOME MONSTERS.
MINAS TUROC! MELENKURION ABATHA!
KLUDD
URGG URGG
HRAAA
NICE TO HAVE SOME-THING USEFUL TO DO...
HHRRRG
WHMPP
WHDD
NNGUHH

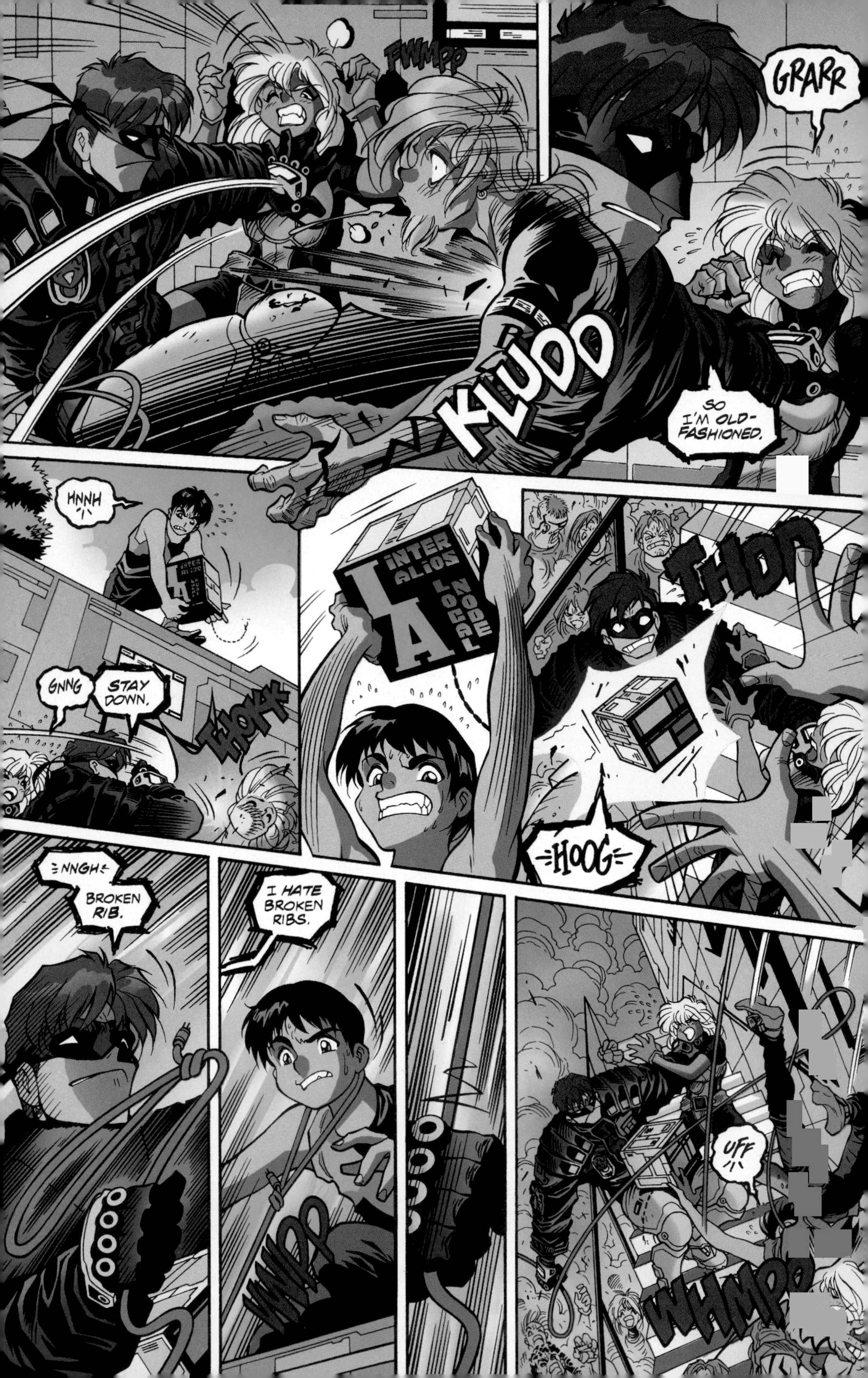
FWMPP
GRARR
KLUDD
SO I'M OLD-FASHIONED.
HNNH
INTER ALIOS LOCAL NODE
THDD
GNNG
STAY DOWN.
THOKK
HOOG
NNGH
BROKEN RIB.
I HATE BROKEN RIBS.
WMPP
UFF
WHMPP

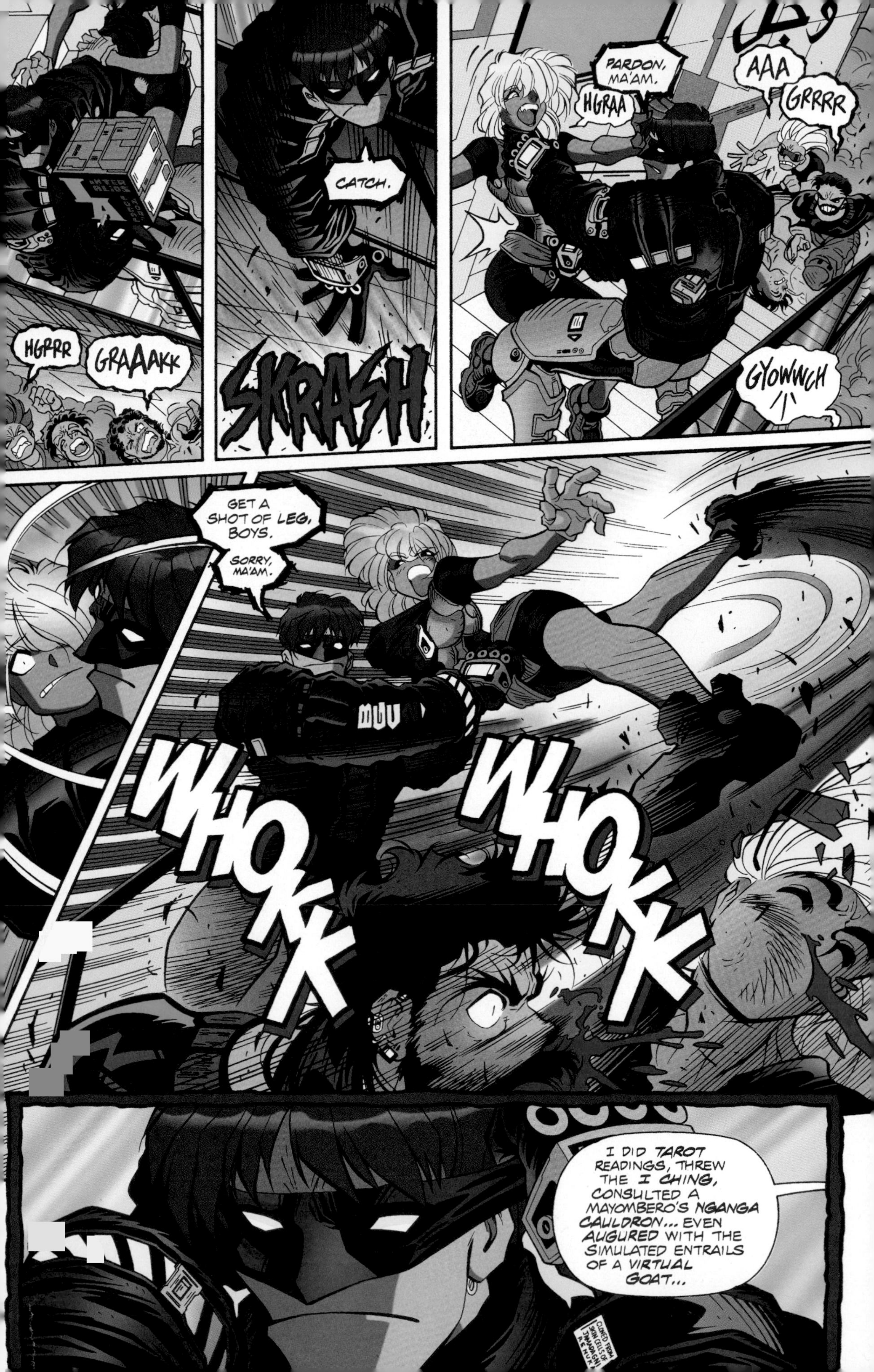
HGRRR
GRAAAKK
CATCH.
SKRASH
PARDON, MA'AM.
HGRAA
AAA
GRRRR
GYOWWCH
GET A SHOT OF LEG, BOYS.
SORRY, MA'AM.
WHOKK
WHOKK
I DID TAROT READINGS, THREW THE I CHING, CONSULTED A MAYOMBERO'S NGANGA CAULDRON... EVEN AUGURED WITH THE SIMULATED ENTRAILS OF A VIRTUAL GOAT...

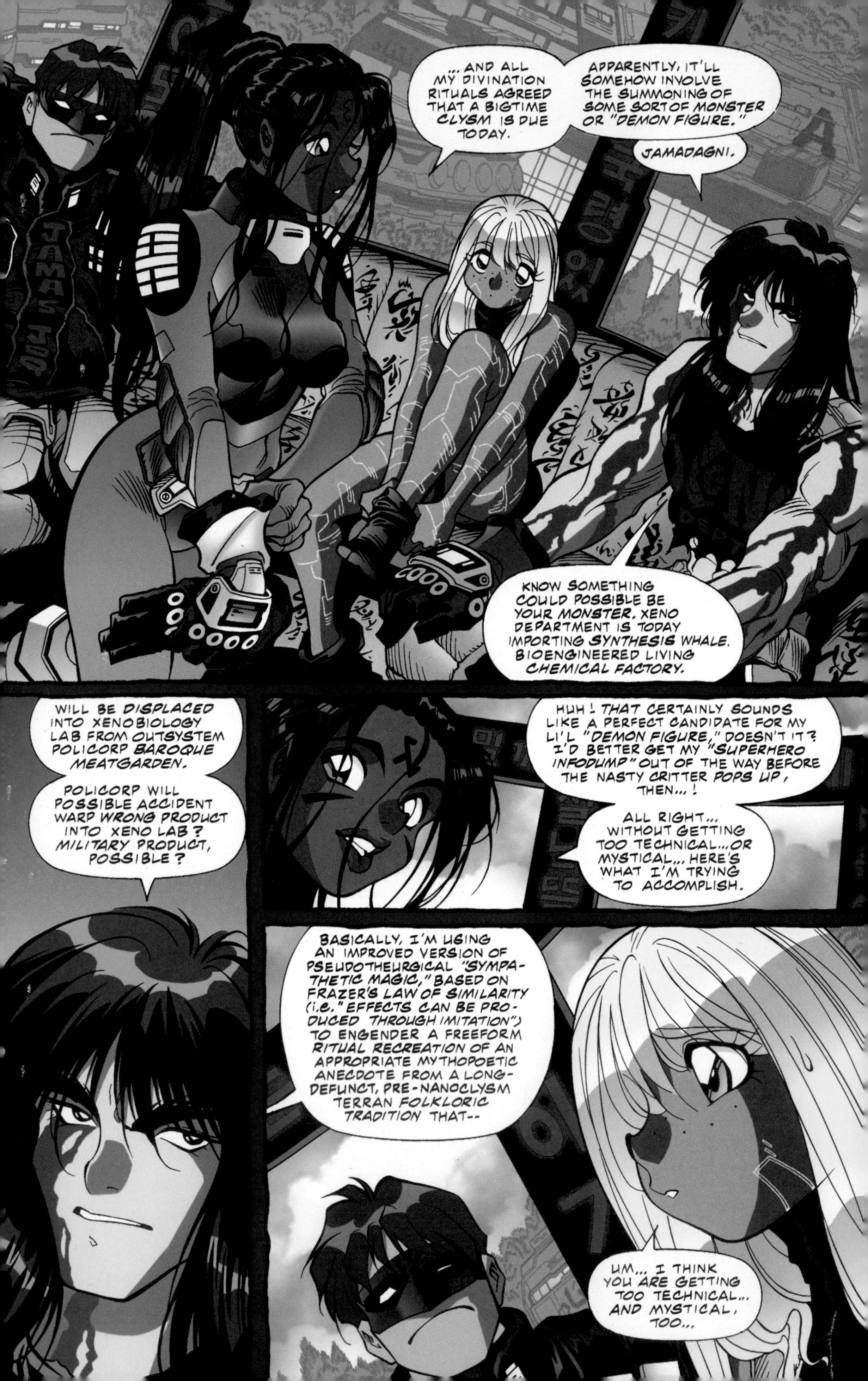

...AND ALL MY DIVINATION RITUALS AGREED THAT A BIGTIME CLYSM IS DUE TODAY.
APPARENTLY, IT'LL SOMEHOW INVOLVE THE SUMMONING OF SOME SORT OF MONSTER OR "DEMON FIGURE."
JAMADAGNI.
KNOW SOMETHING COULD POSSIBLE BE YOUR MONSTER. XENO DEPARTMENT IS TODAY IMPORTING SYNTHESIS WHALE. BIOENGINEERED LIVING CHEMICAL FACTORY.
WILL BE DISPLACED INTO XENOBIOLOGY LAB FROM OUTSYSTEM POLICORP BAROQUE MEATGARDEN.
POLICORP WILL POSSIBLE ACCIDENT WARP WRONG PRODUCT INTO XENO LAB? MILITARY PRODUCT, POSSIBLE?
HUH! THAT CERTAINLY SOUNDS LIKE A PERFECT CANDIDATE FOR MY LI'L "DEMON FIGURE," DOESN'T IT? I'D BETTER GET MY "SUPERHERO INFODUMP" OUT OF THE WAY BEFORE THE NASTY CRITTER POPS UP, THEN...!
ALL RIGHT... WITHOUT GETTING TOO TECHNICAL...OR MYSTICAL... HERE'S WHAT I'M TRYING TO ACCOMPLISH.
BASICALLY, I'M USING AN IMPROVED VERSION OF PSEUDOTHEURGICAL "SYMPATHETIC MAGIC," BASED ON FRAZER'S LAW OF SIMILARITY (i.e. "EFFECTS CAN BE PRODUCED THROUGH IMITATION") TO ENGENDER A FREEFORM RITUAL RECREATION OF AN APPROPRIATE MYTHOPOETIC ANECDOTE FROM A LONG-DEFUNCT, PRE-NANOCLYSM TERRAN FOLKLORIC TRADITION THAT--
UM... I THINK YOU ARE GETTING TOO TECHNICAL... AND MYSTICAL, TOO...

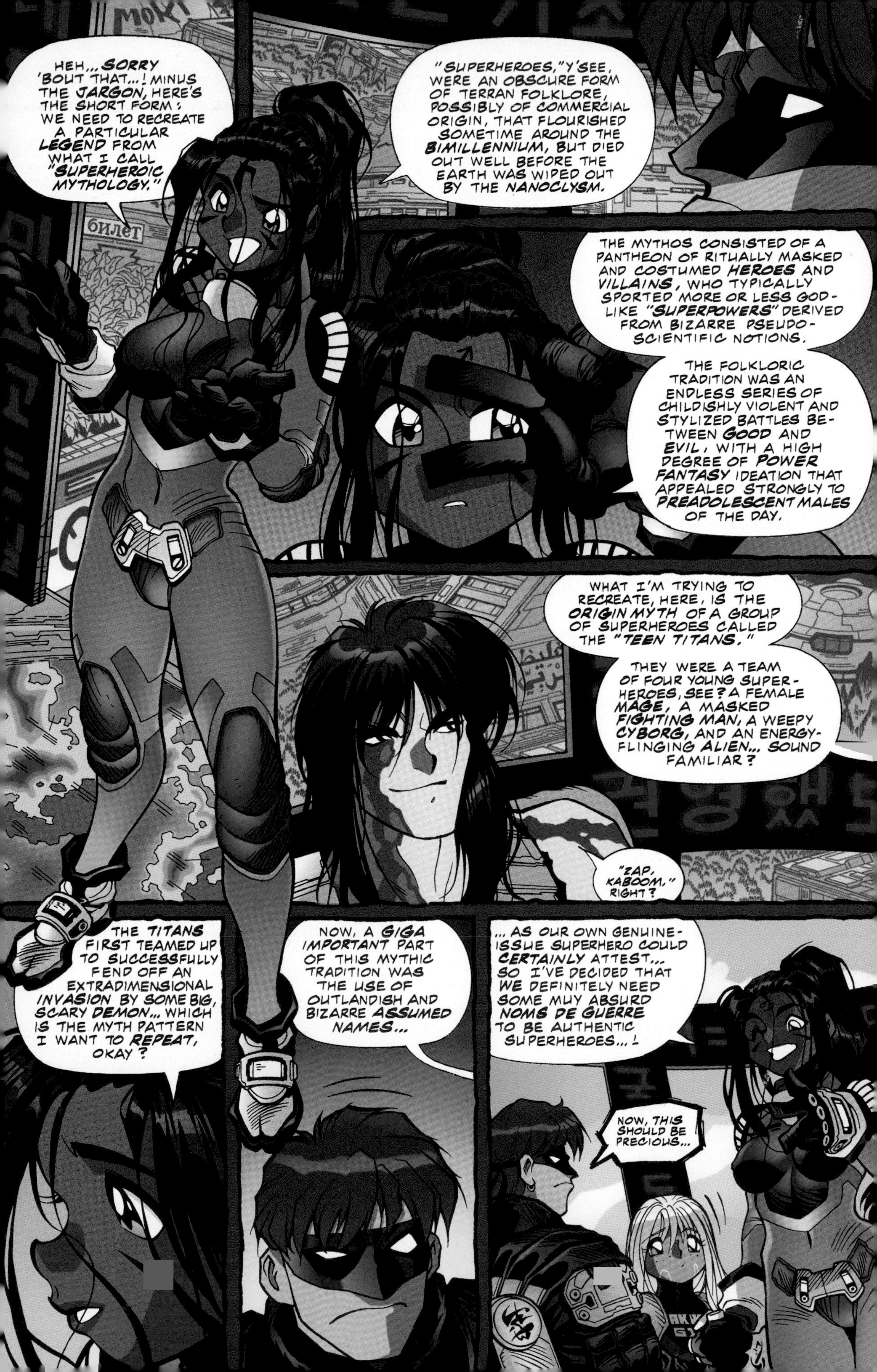
HEH... SORRY 'BOUT THAT...! MINUS THE JARGON, HERE'S THE SHORT FORM: WE NEED TO RECREATE A PARTICULAR LEGEND FROM WHAT I CALL "SUPERHEROIC MYTHOLOGY."
"SUPERHEROES," Y'SEE, WERE AN OBSCURE FORM OF TERRAN FOLKLORE, POSSIBLY OF COMMERCIAL ORIGIN, THAT FLOURISHED SOMETIME AROUND THE BIMILLENNIUM, BUT DIED OUT WELL BEFORE THE EARTH WAS WIPED OUT BY THE NANOCLYSM.
билет
THE MYTHOS CONSISTED OF A PANTHEON OF RITUALLY MASKED AND COSTUMED HEROES AND VILLAINS, WHO TYPICALLY SPORTED MORE OR LESS GOD-LIKE "SUPERPOWERS" DERIVED FROM BIZARRE PSEUDO-SCIENTIFIC NOTIONS.
THE FOLKLORIC TRADITION WAS AN ENDLESS SERIES OF CHILDISHLY VIOLENT AND STYLIZED BATTLES BETWEEN GOOD AND EVIL, WITH A HIGH DEGREE OF POWER FANTASY IDEATION THAT APPEALED STRONGLY TO PREADOLESCENT MALES OF THE DAY.
WHAT I'M TRYING TO RECREATE, HERE, IS THE ORIGIN MYTH OF A GROUP OF SUPERHEROES CALLED THE "TEEN TITANS."
THEY WERE A TEAM OF FOUR YOUNG SUPER-HEROES, SEE? A FEMALE MAGE, A MASKED FIGHTING MAN, A WEEPY CYBORG, AND AN ENERGY-FLINGING ALIEN... SOUND FAMILIAR?
"ZAP, KABOOM," RIGHT?
THE TITANS FIRST TEAMED UP TO SUCCESSFULLY FEND OFF AN EXTRADIMENSIONAL INVASION BY SOME BIG, SCARY DEMON... WHICH IS THE MYTH PATTERN I WANT TO REPEAT, OKAY?
NOW, A GIGA IMPORTANT PART OF THIS MYTHIC TRADITION WAS THE USE OF OUTLANDISH AND BIZARRE ASSUMED NAMES...
...AS OUR OWN GENUINE-ISSUE SUPERHERO COULD CERTAINLY ATTEST... SO I'VE DECIDED THAT WE DEFINITELY NEED SOME MUY ABSURD NOMS DE GUERRE TO BE AUTHENTIC SUPERHEROES...!
NOW, THIS SHOULD BE PRECIOUS...

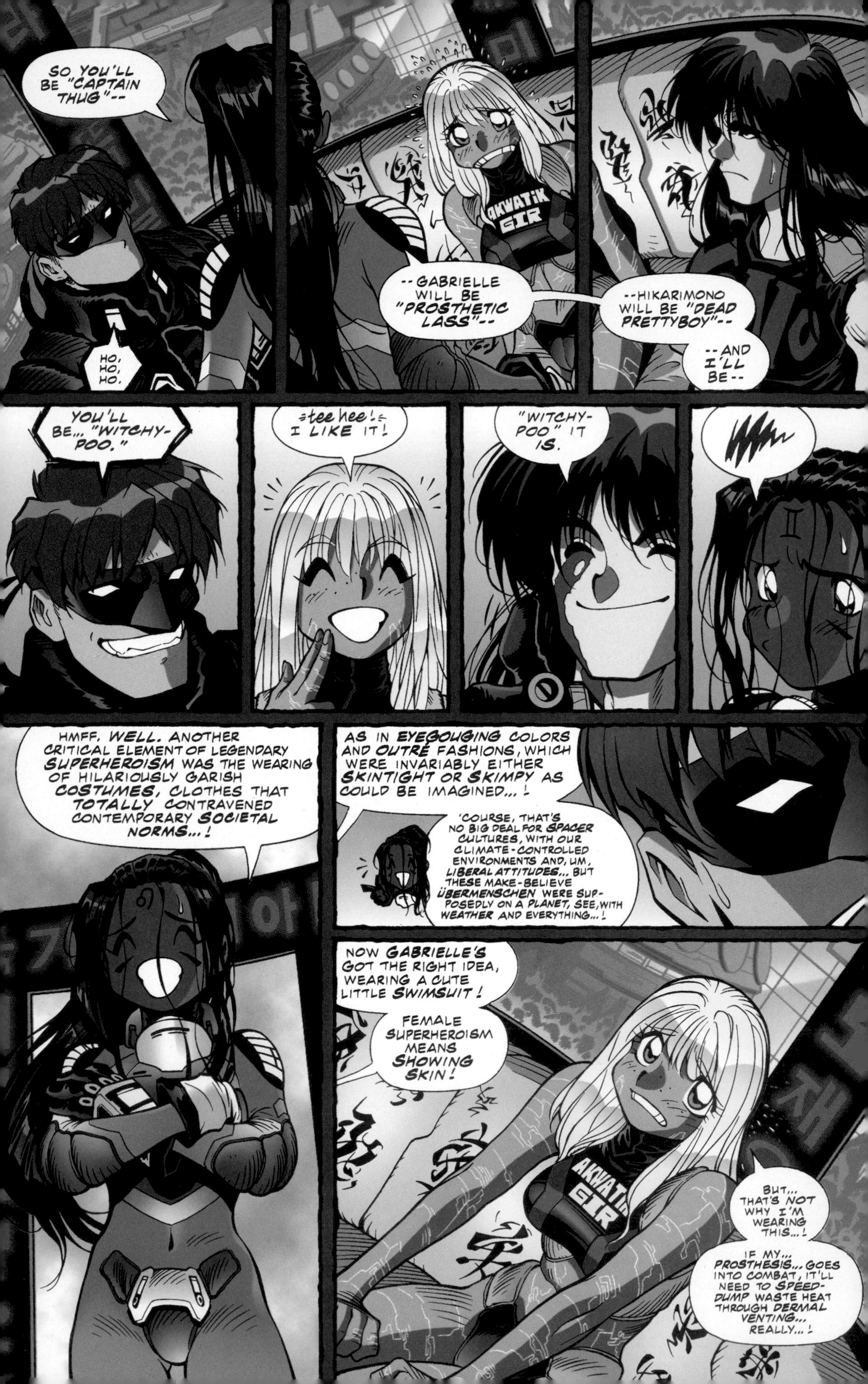
SO YOU'LL BE "CAPTAIN THUG"--
HO, HO, HO.
--GABRIELLE WILL BE "PROSTHETIC LASS"--
--HIKARIMONO WILL BE "DEAD PRETTYBOY"--
--AND I'LL BE--
YOU'LL BE... "WITCHY-POO."
tee hee! I LIKE IT!
"WITCHY-POO" IT IS.
HMFF. WELL. ANOTHER CRITICAL ELEMENT OF LEGENDARY SUPERHEROISM WAS THE WEARING OF HILARIOUSLY GARISH COSTUMES, CLOTHES THAT TOTALLY CONTRAVENED CONTEMPORARY SOCIETAL NORMS...!
AS IN EYEGOUGING COLORS AND OUTRÉ FASHIONS, WHICH WERE INVARIABLY EITHER SKINTIGHT OR SKIMPY AS COULD BE IMAGINED...!
'COURSE, THAT'S NO BIG DEAL FOR SPACER CULTURES, WITH OUR CLIMATE-CONTROLLED ENVIRONMENTS AND, UM, LIBERAL ATTITUDES... BUT THESE MAKE-BELIEVE ÜBERMENSCHEN WERE SUPPOSEDLY ON A PLANET, SEE, WITH WEATHER AND EVERYTHING...!
NOW GABRIELLE'S GOT THE RIGHT IDEA, WEARING A CUTE LITTLE SWIMSUIT!
FEMALE SUPERHEROISM MEANS SHOWING SKIN!
BUT... THAT'S NOT WHY I'M WEARING THIS...!
IF MY... PROSTHESIS... GOES INTO COMBAT, IT'LL NEED TO SPEED-DUMP WASTE HEAT THROUGH DERMAL VENTING... REALLY...!

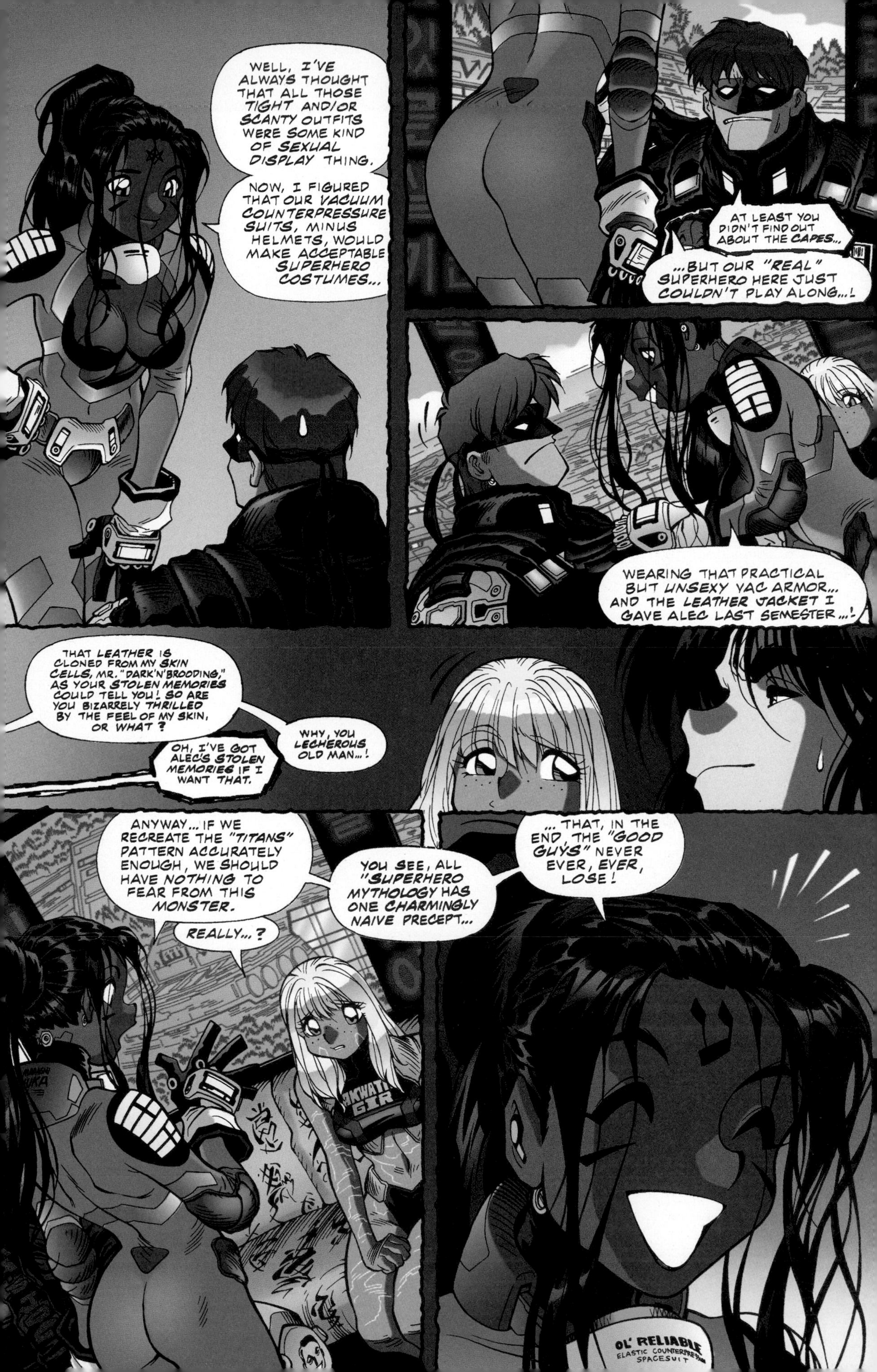

WELL, I'VE ALWAYS THOUGHT THAT ALL THOSE TIGHT AND/OR SCANTY OUTFITS WERE SOME KIND OF SEXUAL DISPLAY THING.
NOW, I FIGURED THAT OUR VACUUM COUNTERPRESSURE SUITS, MINUS HELMETS, WOULD MAKE ACCEPTABLE SUPERHERO COSTUMES...
AT LEAST YOU DIDN'T FIND OUT ABOUT THE CAPES...
...BUT OUR "REAL" SUPERHERO HERE JUST COULDN'T PLAY ALONG...!
WEARING THAT PRACTICAL BUT UNSEXY VAC ARMOR... AND THE LEATHER JACKET I GAVE ALEC LAST SEMESTER...!
THAT LEATHER IS CLONED FROM MY SKIN CELLS, MR. "DARK'N'BROODING," AS YOUR STOLEN MEMORIES COULD TELL YOU! SO ARE YOU BIZARRELY THRILLED BY THE FEEL OF MY SKIN, OR WHAT?
WHY, YOU LECHEROUS OLD MAN...!
OH, I'VE GOT ALEC'S STOLEN MEMORIES IF I WANT THAT.
ANYWAY... IF WE RECREATE THE "TITANS" PATTERN ACCURATELY ENOUGH, WE SHOULD HAVE NOTHING TO FEAR FROM THIS MONSTER.
REALLY...?
YOU SEE, ALL "SUPERHERO MYTHOLOGY HAS ONE CHARMINGLY NAIVE PRECEPT...
... THAT, IN THE END, THE "GOOD GUYS" NEVER EVER, EVER, LOSE!
OL' RELIABLE
ELASTIC COUNTERPRESSURE SPACESUIT

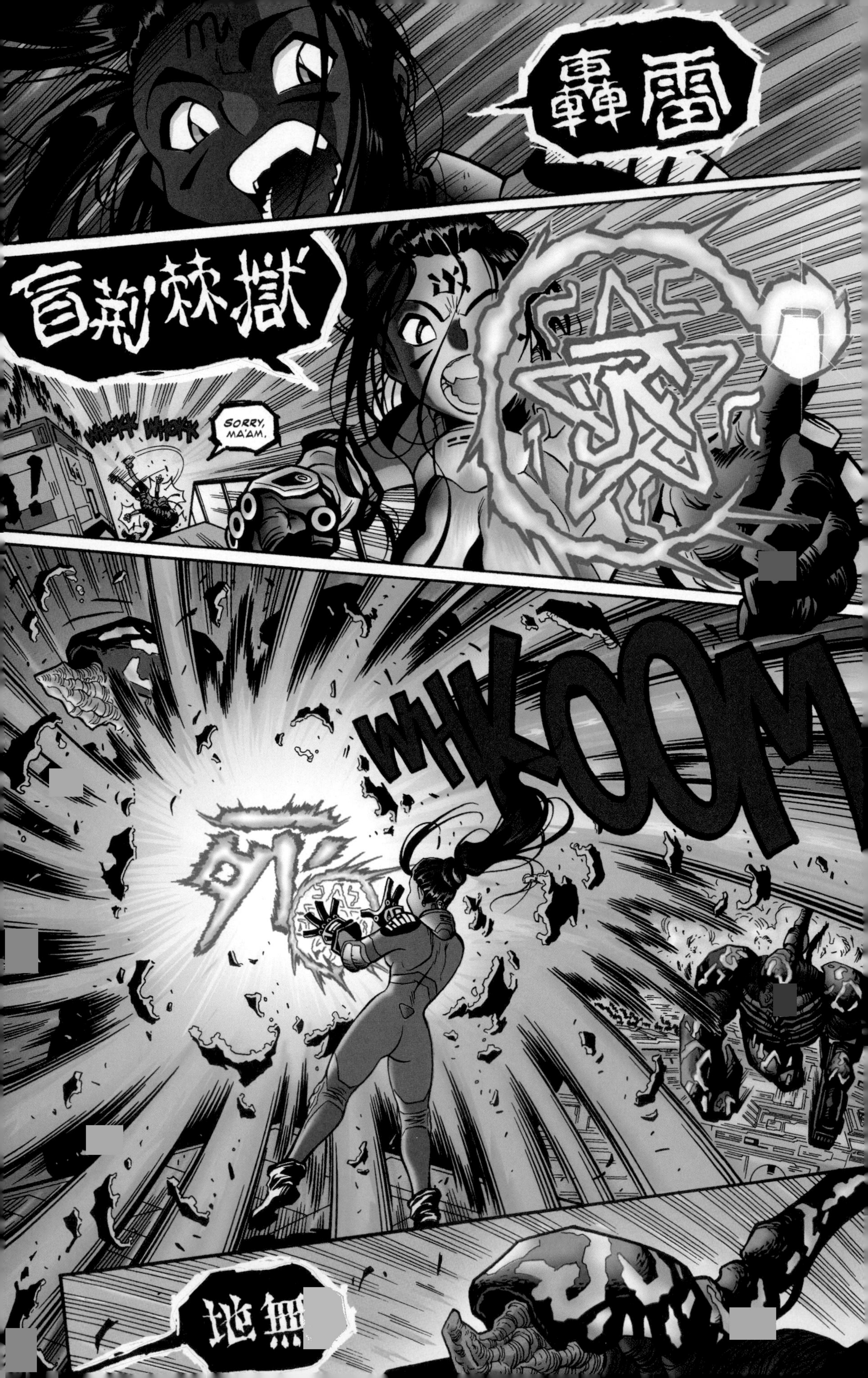

轟雷
盲荊棘獄
WHOKK WHOKK
SORRY, MA'AM.
WHKOOM
地無

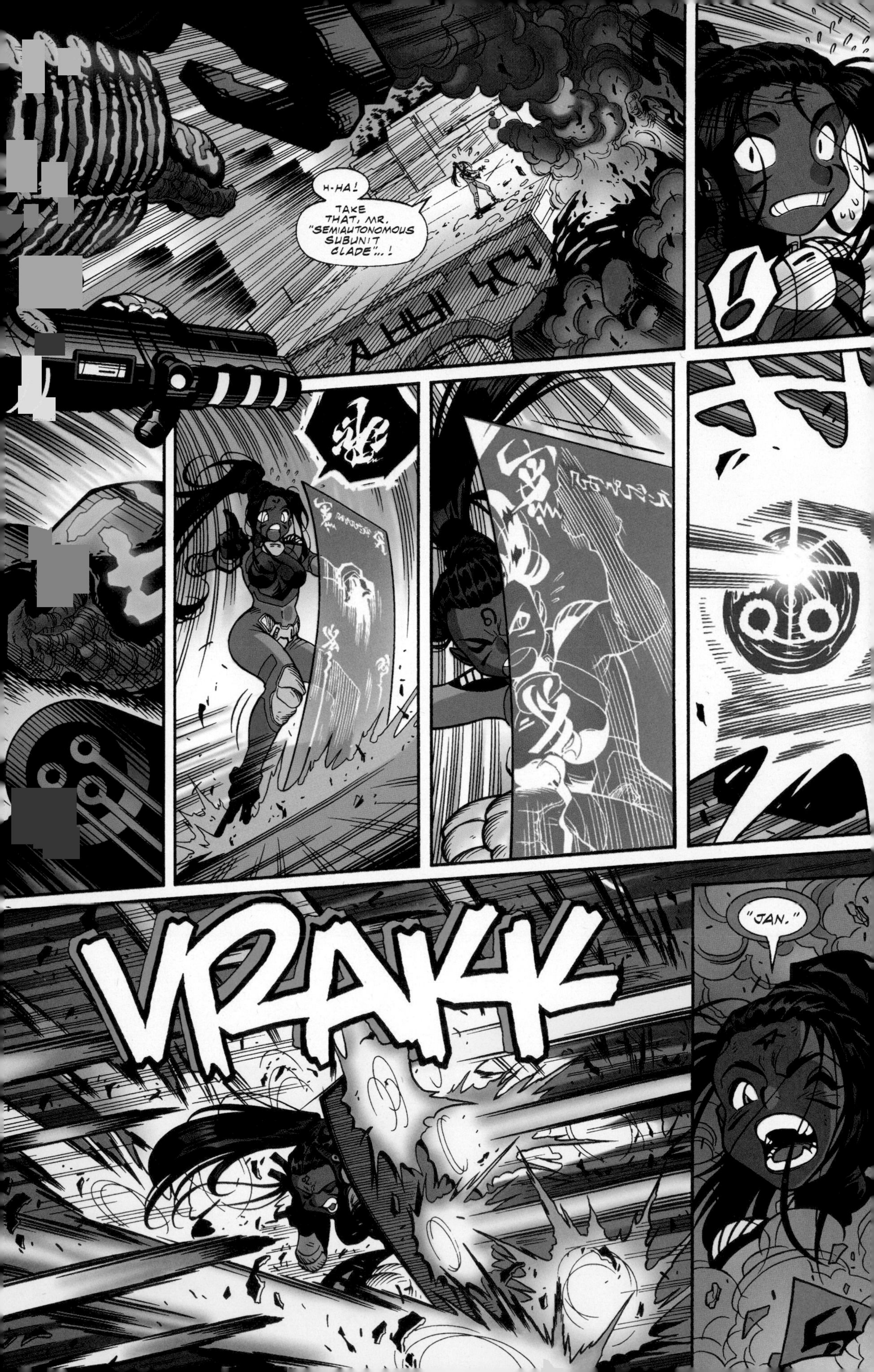
H-HA!
TAKE THAT, MR. "SEMIAUTONOMOUS SUBUNIT CLADE"...!
VRAKK
"JAN."

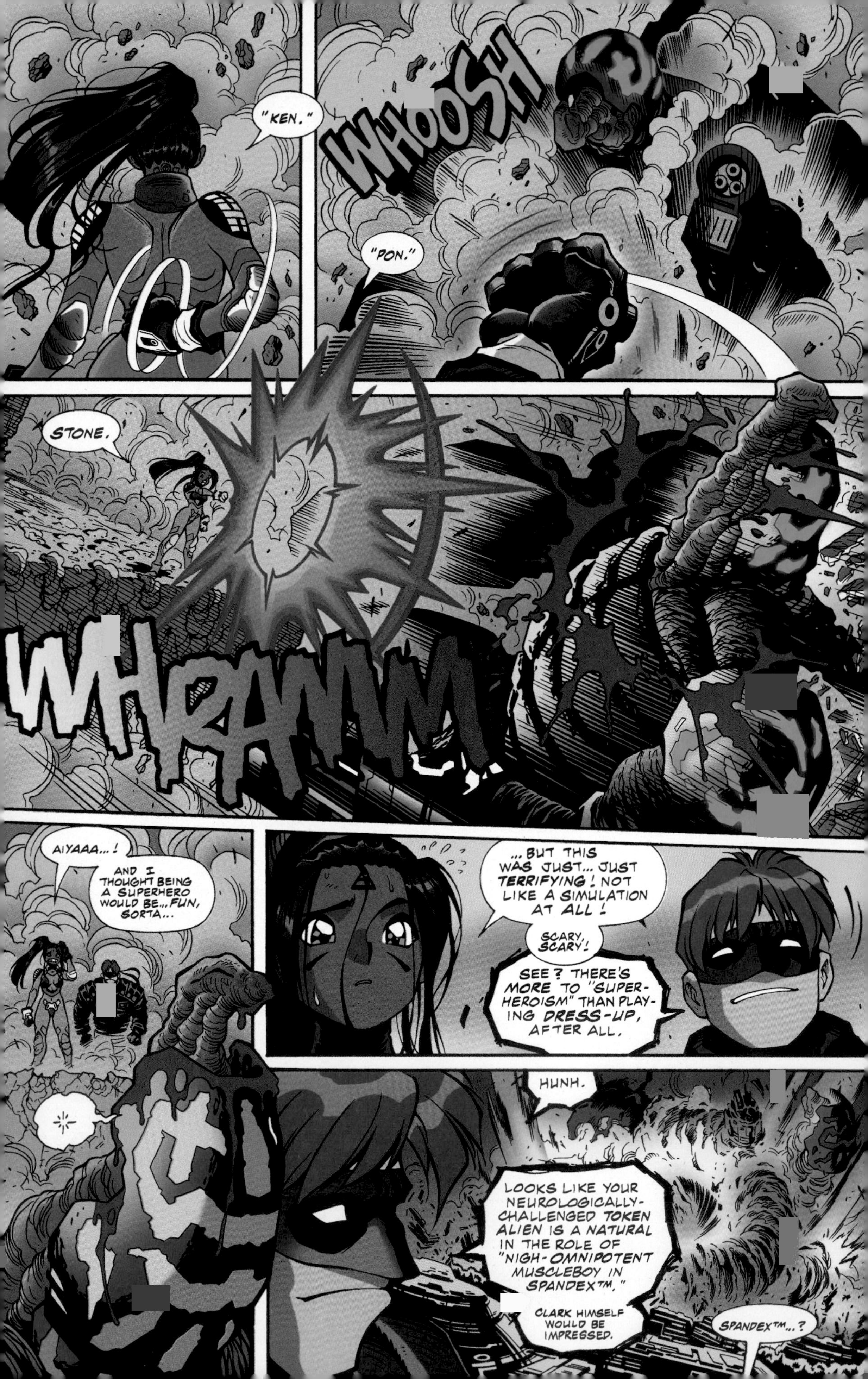
"KEN."
WHOOSH
"PON."
STONE.
WHRAMM
AIYAAA...!
AND I THOUGHT BEING A SUPERHERO WOULD BE...FUN, SORTA...
...BUT THIS WAS JUST... JUST TERRIFYING! NOT LIKE A SIMULATION AT ALL!
SCARY, SCARY!
SEE? THERE'S MORE TO "SUPER-HEROISM" THAN PLAY-ING DRESS-UP, AFTER ALL.
HUNH.
LOOKS LIKE YOUR NEUROLOGICALLY-CHALLENGED TOKEN ALIEN IS A NATURAL IN THE ROLE OF "NIGH-OMNIPOTENT MUSCLEBOY IN SPANDEX™."
CLARK HIMSELF WOULD BE IMPRESSED.
SPANDEX™...?

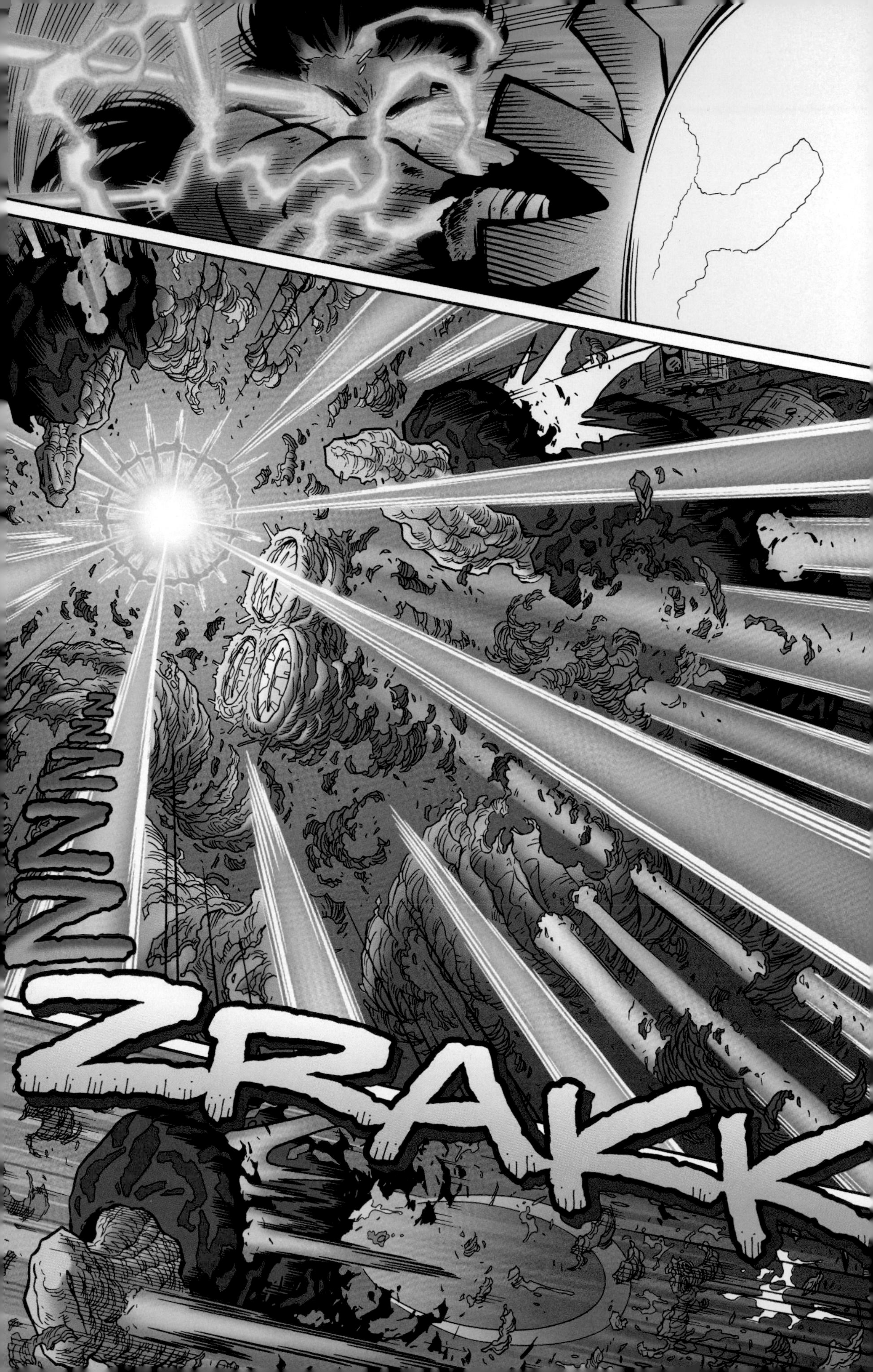
NNNNNN
ZRAKK

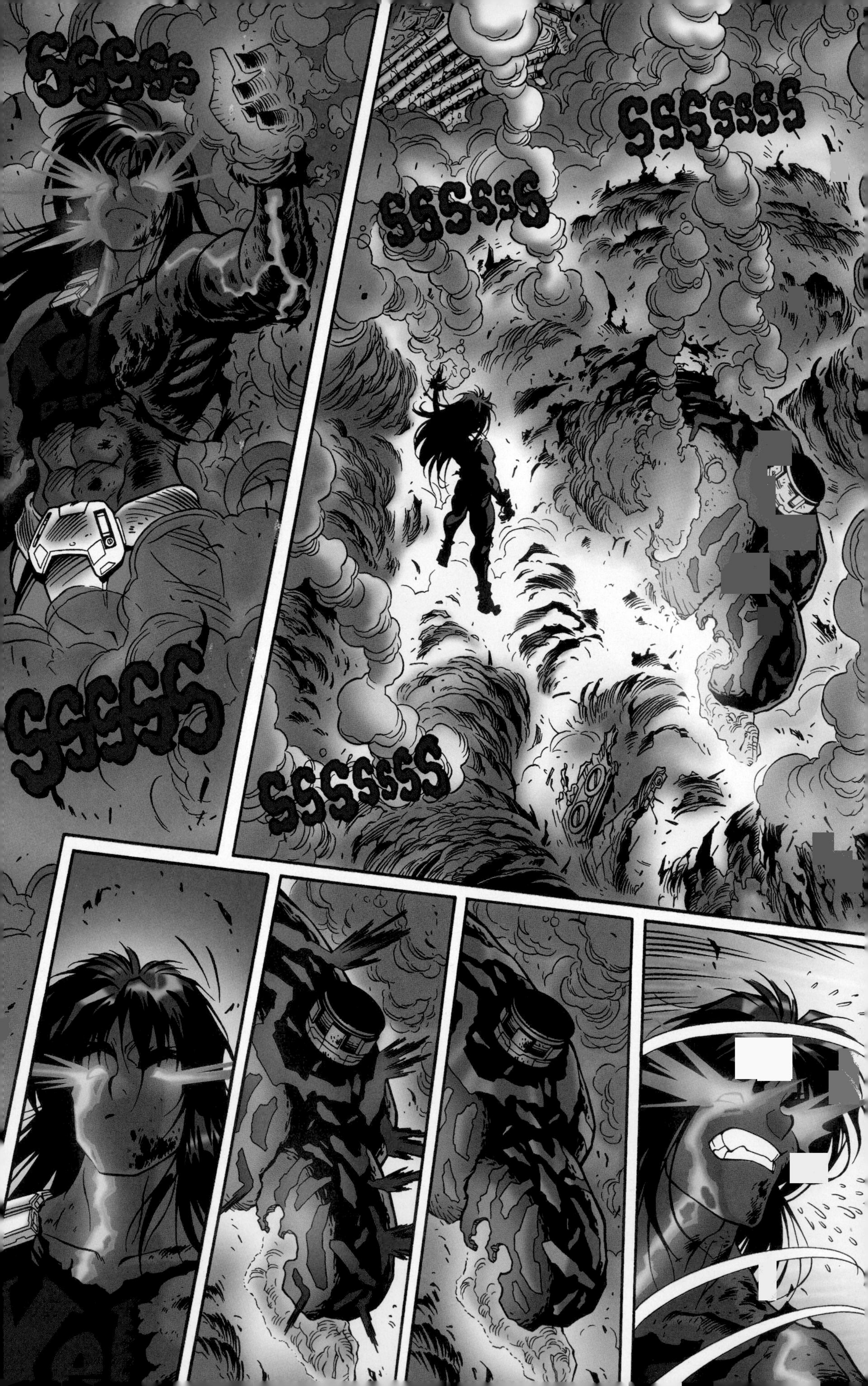
SSSSSS
SSSSSS
SSSSSS
SSSSSSS
SSSSSSS

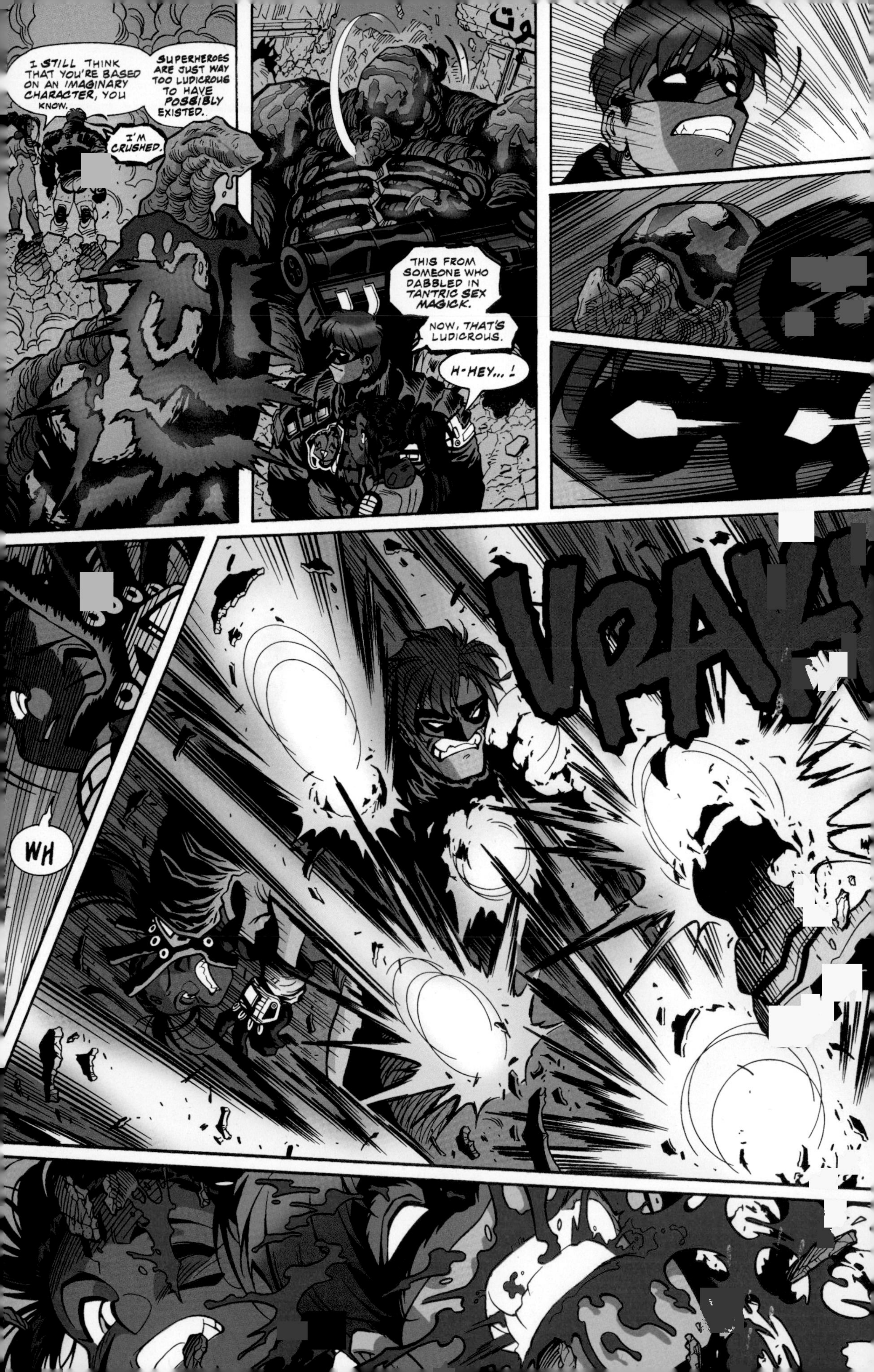
I STILL THINK THAT YOU'RE BASED ON AN IMAGINARY CHARACTER, YOU KNOW.
SUPERHEROES ARE JUST WAY TOO LUDICROUS TO HAVE POSSIBLY EXISTED.
I'M CRUSHED.
THIS FROM SOMEONE WHO DABBLED IN TANTRIC SEX MAGICK.
NOW, THAT'S LUDICROUS.
H-HEY...!
WH

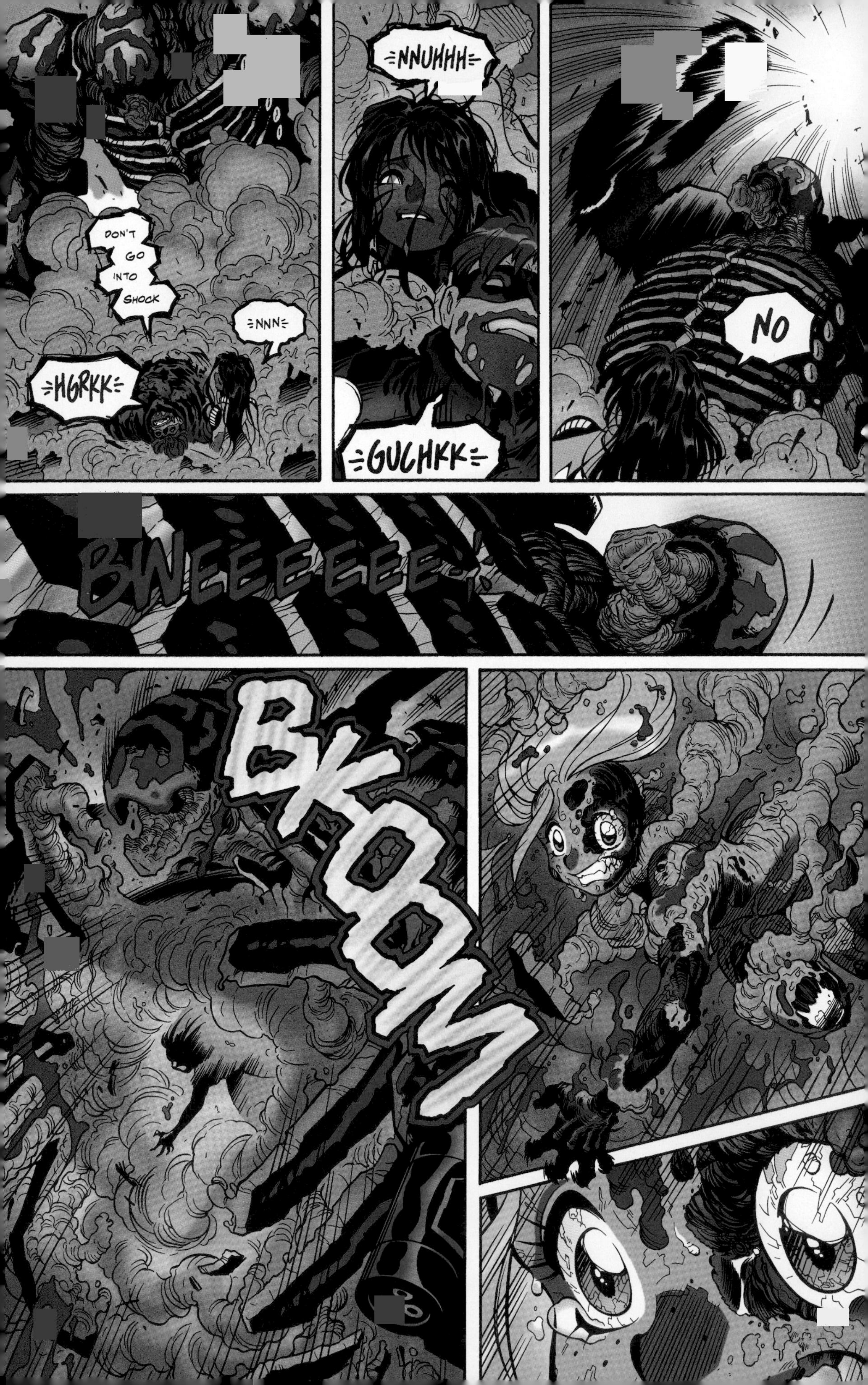
DON'T GO INTO SHOCK
NNN
HGRKK
NNUHHH
GUCHKK
NO
BWEEEEEE
BKOOM

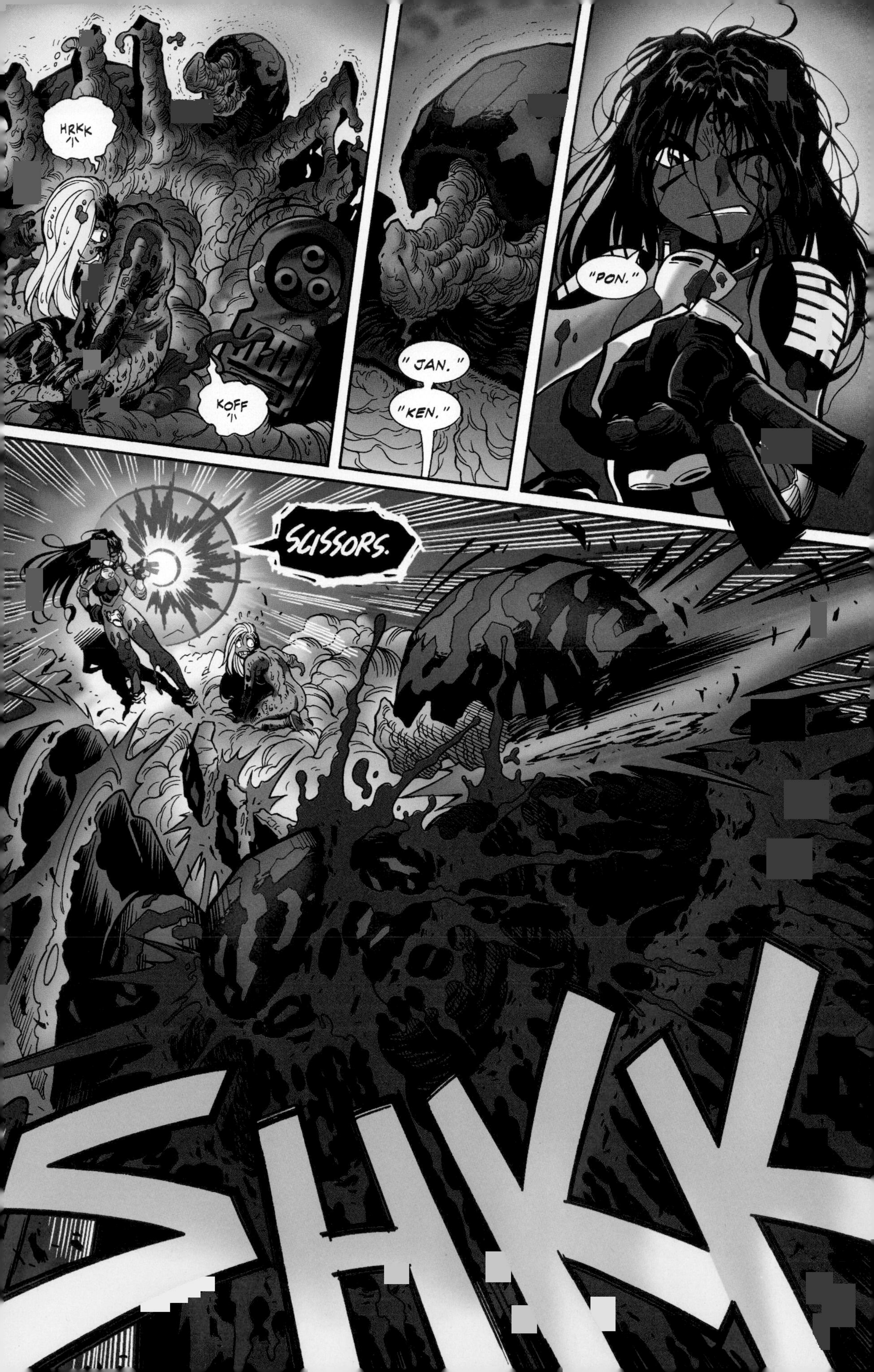
HRKK
KOFF
"JAN."
"KEN."
"PON."
SCISSORS.
SHKK

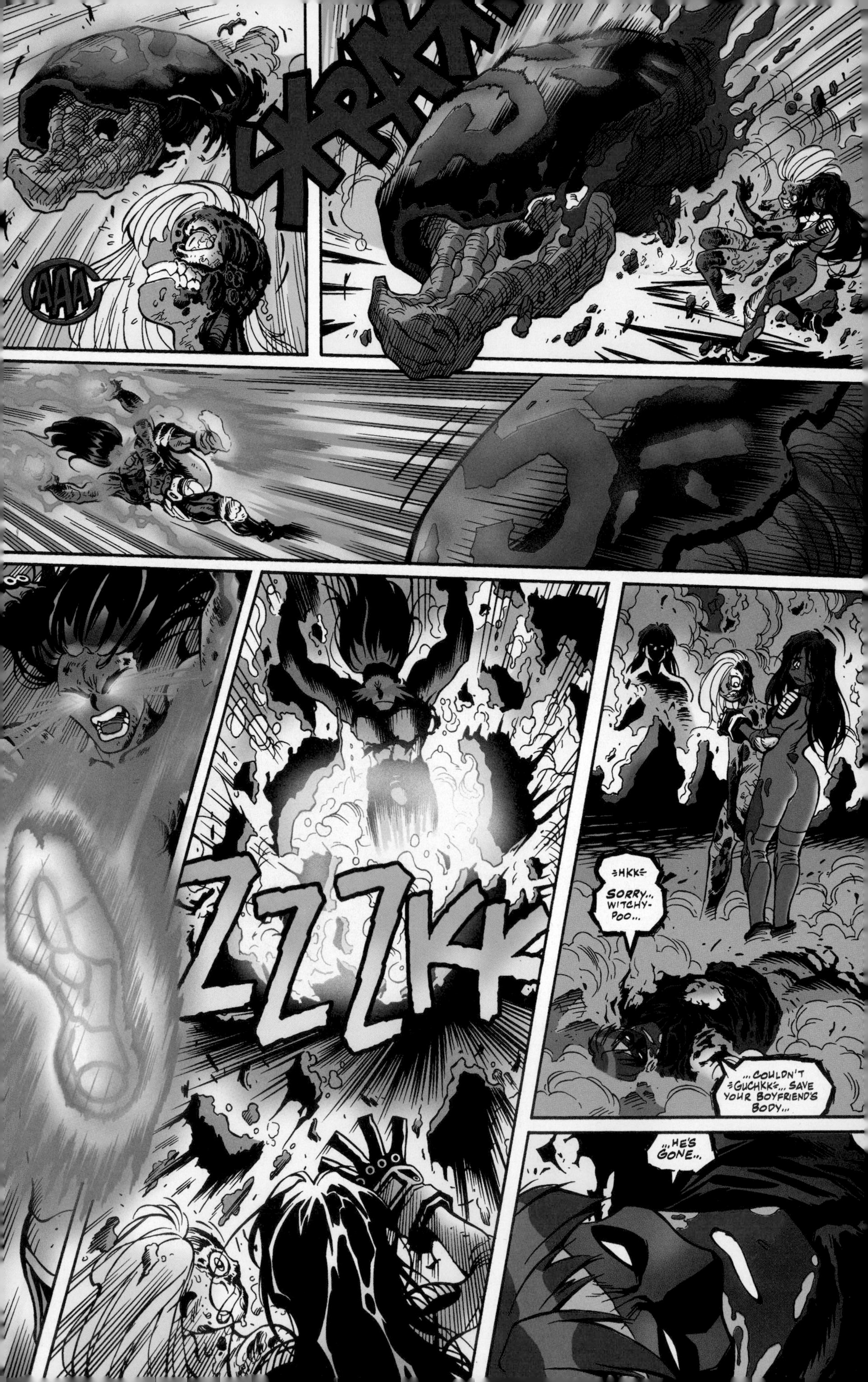
AAA
KRAKT
ZZZK
HKK
SORRY... WITCHY-POO...
...COULDN'T GUCHKK... SAVE YOUR BOYFRIEND'S BODY...
...HE'S GONE...

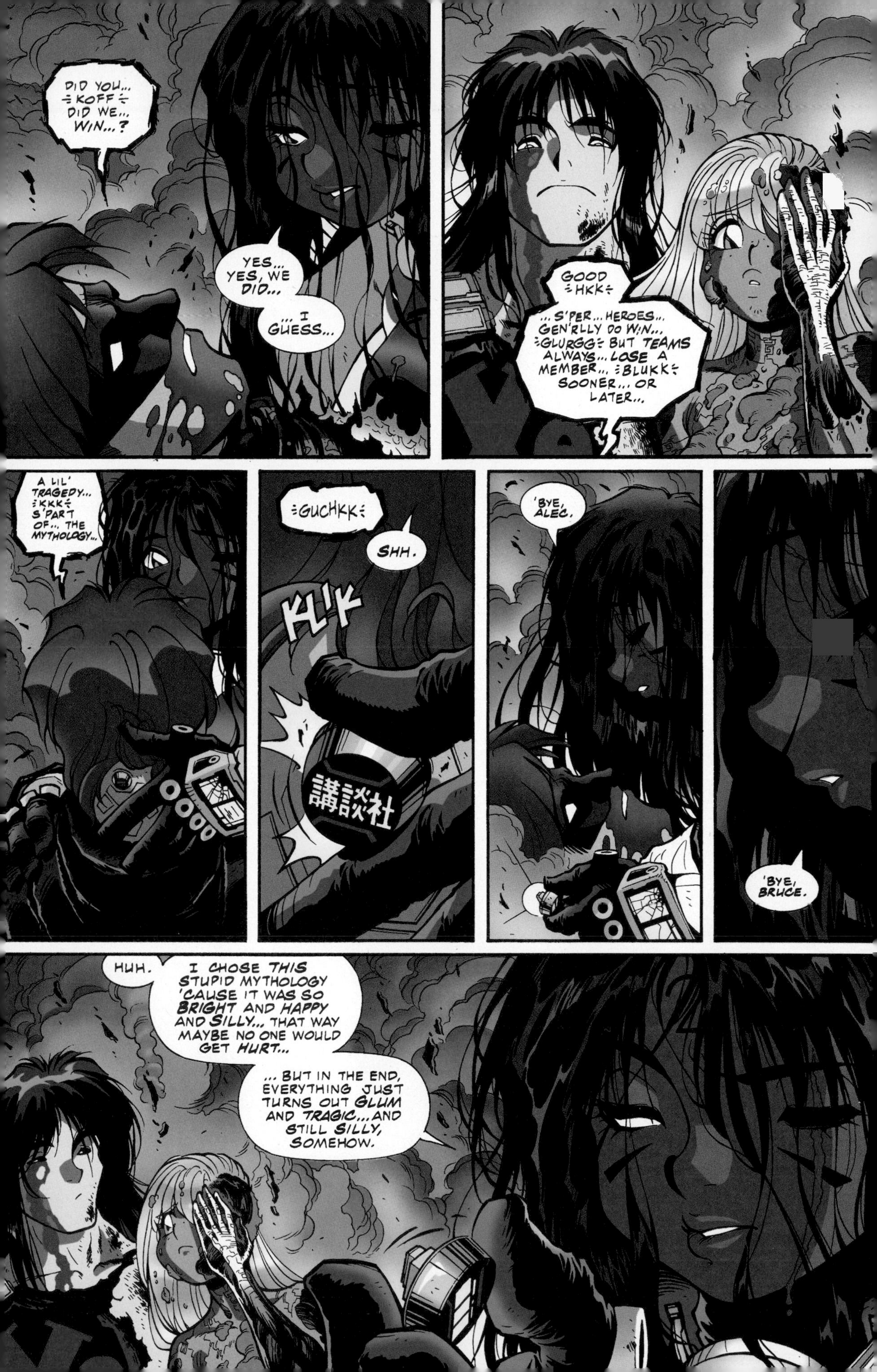

DID YOU... ≑KOFF≑ DID WE... WIN...?
YES... YES, WE DID...
...I GUESS...
GOOD ≑HKK≑
...S'PER... HEROES... GEN'RLLY DO WIN... ≑GLURGG≑ BUT TEAMS ALWAYS... LOSE A MEMBER... ≑BLUKK≑ SOONER... OR LATER...
A LIL' TRAGEDY... ≑KKK≑ S'PART OF... THE MYTHOLOGY...
≑GUCHKK≑
SHH.
KLIK
講談社
'BYE, ALEC.
'BYE, BRUCE.
HUH.
I CHOSE THIS STUPID MYTHOLOGY 'CAUSE IT WAS SO BRIGHT AND HAPPY AND SILLY... THAT WAY MAYBE NO ONE WOULD GET HURT...
...BUT IN THE END, EVERYTHING JUST TURNS OUT GLUM AND TRAGIC... AND STILL SILLY, SOMEHOW.

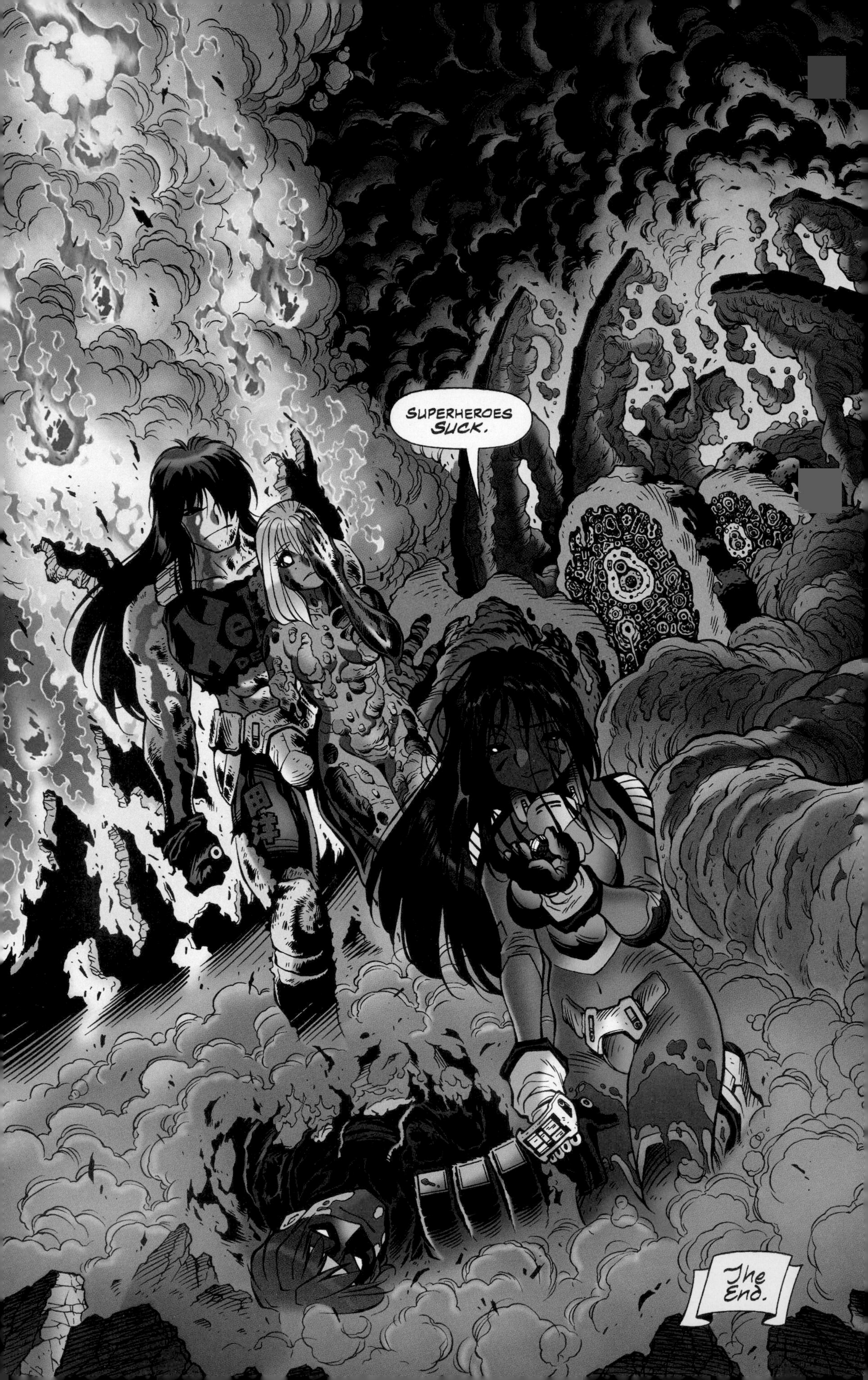
SUPERHEROES SUCK.
The End.